Price of Fame

Amaleka McCall

URBAN
BOOKS

Urban Books, LLC
78 East Industry Court
Deer Park, NY 11729

ISBN 13: 978-1-60162-284-6
ISBN 10: 1-60162-284-8

First Printing October 2010
Printed in the United States of America

10 9 8 7 6 5 4 3 2 1

Distributed by Kensington Publishing Corp.
Submit Wholesale Orders to:
Kensington Publishing Corp.
C/O Penguin Group (USA) Inc.
Attention: Order Processing
405 Murray Hill Parkway
East Rutherford, NJ 07073-2316
Phone: 1-800-526-0275
Fax: 1-800-227-9604

Dedication

To Chynna and Amaya, my beautiful girls.

You both are my constant inspiration. As long as I breathe, I will continue to be a voice for abused girls and women. Mommy loves you both.

"In the future, everyone will be world-famous for fifteen minutes."

Andy Warhol
1968

New York Post
FOURTEEN-YEAR-OLD GIRL FOUND DEAD IN BROOKLYN DUMPSTER

New York Times
POLICE OFFICER DUBBED A HERO AFTER TAKING DOWN TWO ROBBERY SUSPECTS

Smut magazine
BUSTY PORN QUEEN ATTEMPTS SUICIDE ON THE SET OF NEW MOVIE

Daily News
HUMAN TRAFFICKING RING UNCOVERED

Chapter One

Rock Bottom

The first time Casey Pete saw a penis she was five years old.

"How come I don't have a worm in my panties?" Casey asked as she stared into her baby brother's diaper.

Casey remembered the warm smile that had spread across her mother's loving face, but couldn't remember her answer. It had been a long time since Casey had seen her mother. She thought about her almost daily now.

Today was much different than the first time she had encountered the genitalia of the opposite sex.

"Ouch! Get up!" Casey screamed, squirming her body and wiping the stranger's sweat off of her chest and face. Disgusted, but also the star of the show, she didn't hesitate to display her feelings.

"Cut!" the director yelled, looking toward Jordan for an explanation. Jordan threw his hands up in surrender, clenching his jaw. The budget for the film had run over by almost $40,000. Mikey, a world-renowned director in the industry, was not a happy camper.

Jordan scrambled out of the mesh director's chair he had taken up residence in since filming had started. He was too late. Casey had jumped up and was speeding off the set. Shielding her eyes from the bright lights dangling from the ceiling and cranes, she scowled and hurried down the long warehouse hallway.

"I need a fuckin' break!" Casey screamed, her voice cracking. She winced as the speed of her movement caused the chafe that had developed between her legs to make her feel like someone had dragged her bare-naked ass across a concrete highway.

"Jordan, I'm going to my trailer for a second," Casey called out, briskly walking as she wrapped a chenille bathrobe around her body. Murmurs passed among the throngs of men who stood in line, dicks in hand, looking like starving refugees. Casey was what they hungered for; she was their relief package.

Casey rushed by, never looking up. She had seen a lifetime's worth of penises—short, long, wide, skinny, circumcised and uncircumcised. Casey felt shame flash in her chest like a newly lit campfire, with small embers escaping to burn her cheeks red.

Growing up, she had learned the hard way that being touched by a boy was like being bitten by a poisonous snake. Now, at twenty-six years old, she seemed to have become immune to the venom. Where she came from she was surely considered an apostate—a person unworthy of going to heaven or even hell, just unworthy.

Flinging open the door to her dressing room trailer, Casey rushed over to her vanity table searching desperately for her medicine. When none was located, she upturned her purse until all of the contents emptied out onto the floor. Among the mess lay a picture of Casey and her best friend, Diamond. Casey slowly lifted the picture to eye level and a sharp pain gripped her chest. She hadn't seen or heard from Diamond in over a year. Casey had turned her back on Diamond, the only person, aside from her mother, who had ever really loved her. Casey had walked over her friend like a piece of trash on the street. Regret and grief caused her to toss the picture back onto the floor.

"Denver Peaks! Denver Peaks! Denver Peaks!" Hands trembling, Casey listened as the crowd outside started chanting her professional name. She closed her eyes tight. The muffled chants sent chills down her spine. "Fuck!" she screamed, banging her fists on the wobbly little vanity until one of her knuckles started to bleed.

Casey put her head down and rocked back and forth. The chants grew louder. Casey knew that the pussy-hungry crowd anxiously awaited her return. This was going to be her big break; at least that's what Jordan Bleu—her manager/boyfriend—had told her two weeks before. The rumble of the eager fans' screams started to shake the shabby plywood walls of Casey's trailer, rattling the small bottles of polish that were thrown haphazardly atop the chipped wood table.

Casey picked up her favorite fire red lipstick, wound it all the way to the top and rubbed it against her thin lips. The lipstick's matte finish saturated the skin around her entire mouth and chin. She felt like a sad clown even though a beautiful girl gazed back at her in the mirror. Tears welled up under her red-rimmed eyes. Casey snorted back the mucus that threatened to escape her nose.

Bang! Bang! Bang!

Casey jumped at the loud knocks on the door. She looked in the mirror one more time. Tears streamed down her face like rapid waterfalls. Like a mirage in the desert, Casey spotted the bottle of Patrón that Jordan had bought her this morning. She crawled on hands and knees, popped open the top and washed her pain away. Jordan was good at supplying her with what she needed to "stay in the game," as he would put it.

"Casey! What the fuck are you doing in there? Time is money!" Jordan called out from the other side of the door, jiggling the doorknob back and forth. Casey could tell by his tone that he was pissed—his voice always shook a little when he got angry.

She could imagine what he would do if he could get to her right now. Grab her cheeks? Pull her hair? Grab her around the throat? Maybe all, if Jordan felt it would ensure he got his cut. Casey knew she had made Jordan, but solely took the blame herself for her own self-destruction.

"I'm coming!" Casey yelled back, trying to keep the dog at bay. "Fucking nuisance," she mumbled. Casey always grew a big fat set of balls when she was alone out of Jordan's earshot.

Casey spotted the small tan pill bottle lying among the mess on the floor. She surveyed its contents, closed her eyes and dumped about fifty tiny blue Vicodin into her mouth. She gagged as some of the pills tumbled awkwardly down her throat. Casey knew the effects the pills had on her. She'd been taking them so often now to dull the aching pain she felt each time she performed. Maybe an entire bottle would do the trick this time. "Diamond, you are a girl's best friend. I am so sorry I betrayed you," Casey uttered aloud, as if her words would somehow reach Diamond's ears. Casey didn't know if Diamond was dead or alive, but based on her last encounter with Diamond, she knew her friend would have preferred the former rather than the latter.

"Casey! I'm not joking, open the fucking door!" Jordan barked, his voice a near shriek.

Moving her blond hair extensions aside, Casey looked at her face once more. She smiled halfheartedly. "Paris Hilton, huh?" Casey mumbled, repeating what a guy had called her the night before. Lots of people told her she looked like Paris Hilton. Looking at herself again, Casey ran the back of her hand across her wet mouth. The lipstick had run down her chin and cheeks to her neck. She looked like Dracula, or at least someone capable of sucking the life out of another. Her black mascara streaked from the corners of her eyes, mixing with the tears and foundation, making a cakey mess of her usually flawless face. Her crystal blue eyes looked a cold shade of grey, clouded with sadness.

"If you're mad about earlier, I apologize," Jordan said, putting his face up against the door, trying to cajole his way in. Casey saw through the bullshit. Casey felt her breathing becoming labored and her muscles begin to relax. That's what she craved—relaxation, ease.

"Mmmmm," Casey moaned. The pills were taking effect. She attempted to lift her hand to her head, but couldn't feel her hand. Her entire body was numb. Yes, that was even better. Casey's head rocked back and forth as her body fought to stay conscious. Her breathing became labored and her lungs painfully contracted. Her heart thumped wildly. Casey could hear her mother's voice, sweet and low in her ears, chanting parables from their book.

Maybe Casey didn't want to die after all. Maybe a Fuck Fest wasn't the worst that she could've done. Just thinking about over two hundred guys having sex with her one after another just for entertainment made Casey sick. The night Jordan introduced the idea to her, Casey screamed at him. She'd done a lot of things since getting into the business, including being with Jordan, including being an accessory to murder, but the most guys she'd taken on at one time was four. Of course, Jordan had coaxed her into it, just like he'd convinced her to turn on Diamond.

"Jord . . ." Casey whispered from the floor. Maybe he could save her. She could still hear her industry name being chanted in the background. The natives were restless indeed. This event had been advertised at all of the major porn stores in

Los Angeles. "Denver Peaks will take you to new heights!" the slogans read. She was slated to have every opening in her body filled with a penis or some object.

"Help," Casey whimpered. She felt herself slipping from existence. She couldn't control her body parts, nor could she keep her eyes open. Extending her arms, Casey made a futile attempt to shake the demon that seemed to be controlling her body.

"Casey! What the fuck is going on in there? Casey!" Jordan screamed, banging his body up against the door.

Dominique sat at her kitchen table, staring out the huge glass patio doors. The sun was shining and the grass was a beautiful shade of jade. Dominique had never imagined her life would turn out this way; she had thanked God several times a day for her good fortune. When she thought about where she came from and where she was now, something Mama Grady had said to her came to mind: "Listen girl, don't you ever settle for the lesser of two evils. Evil is evil, no matter what the packaging looks like."

Dominique often wondered if she'd indeed chosen the lesser of two evils with the life she had now. She missed those little jewels of wisdom from Mama Grady, who had taken care of Dominique when she was at some of the lowest points in her life. How proud Mama Grady would be if she could see her now.

A toilet flushed upstairs. Dominique glanced at the clock on the wall oven of her gourmet kitchen and almost choked on her coffee. "Shoot," she mumbled, rushing up from the table, making sure not to leave one crumb or spill in her wake. It was already about ten minutes past Dominique's schedule.

Today's breakfast needed to be extra special. As with everything she did, Dominique made sure to put in 110 percent. It was a big day at the church for her husband, Alton, who would be delivering his most important sermon to a congregation of over three thousand and a visiting church. Breakfast had to be just right to ensure his day went well.

Dominique jumped at the sound of her cell phone ringing. Not too many people had the number, and someone calling her at 8:00 A.M.. would surely send off a red flag if Alton heard it.

"Hello," she whispered, trying to intercept the call.

"Diamond?" the man's voice rasped on the other end. Dominique's heart pounded in her chest. She furrowed her brow and removed the phone from her ear to look at the small screen that displayed the word "unknown."

"Diamond?" the voice inquired again. A flash of heat came over her body and her hands shook. She had recognized the voice. How could she forget it? A stabbing pain shot through her abdomen as her bowels threatened to release.

"What do you want?" she asked nervously, keeping her eyes peeled for signs of Alton.

"It's Jordan. I'm calling about Denver . . . I mean, Casey . . . um. Something has happened to her." Jordan stumbled over his words. The call was equally awkward for both of them.

Dominique closed her eyes and held on to the phone so tightly her knuckles turned white. She wanted so badly to hang up, but something inside of her wouldn't allow her to do it. She had expected a call like this to come sooner or later. She could only run from her past for so long. Besides Mama Grady, Dominique still regarded Casey as the only family she'd ever had.

"Diamond? You there?" Jordan asked.

Dominique stood, lost in thought, when Alton's hand touched her shoulder. She visibly jumped from the contact.

"Good morning. Is breakfast ready?" Alton asked, looking strangely at his wife. Dominique knew him so well; she could almost predict what his next question would be, so she stayed one step ahead of him.

"Yes, you can just hold the cake for me and I will be there to pick it up," Dominique said deceptively into the phone.

"What?" Jordan asked, confused.

"Yes, I will be there when you open," Dominique continued, her hands so sweaty she almost lost her grip on the phone.

"Just in case you want to know, she is at Lincoln Hospital fighting for her life," Jordan said with finality before hanging up.

Dominique held the phone to her ear a little longer. Her mind raced with questions and her nerves were rattled, but she managed to pull it together.

"What are you ordering a cake for?" Alton asked suspiciously. Dominique took a deep breath and did her best to calm her nerves.

"It's your big day, baby. I wanted you to have something special," she fabricated on the spot.

"I don't need a cake. I need my wife to get me some breakfast and I am my mother's baby, not yours," Alton said sharply, cracking his knuckles.

"Sorry, I forgot," Dominique said, lowering her eyes as she quickly went about preparing his meal.

Jordan paced the floor of Casey's hospital room. He held his head down as he wore the bottoms of his shoes, pacing up and down cold tile floors. The beeping of the heart monitors was driving Jordan fucking crazy. He wanted to pull every tube out of Casey's body, throw her over his shoulder, and take her home. How sick could she be? They had pumped the pills out of her stomach and she was still alive. Not only was he losing money, he was about to lose the only woman he'd ever really cared about. That probably bothered him the most, but he wouldn't ever admit it.

Jordan had taught himself that money was his only motivation in life. Caring about Casey was something he pushed to the far corners of his mind. But he wouldn't go so far as to call it love. He had decided when he was a kid that love didn't exist; in fact, he considered the word to be as bad as all the other four-letter swear words.

Mikey had vowed that Jordan would pay him back every red cent for the cost of the film production that Casey had fucked up when she decided to commit suicide. What would he do now? With Casey all messed up, there was no telling what would happen to both of their careers. Jordan had worked hard to get himself where he was today. Granted, Casey was the reason for his success, but the fact remained that he was the brain behind the operation.

Jordan had to get his thoughts together, contemplate his next move. He stopped pacing and screwed open his third bottle of Mylanta, put it up to his chapped lips and drank it straight. Beating his chest, Jordan tried to get the burning to stop. With fire in his eyes, he walked over to Casey's bed and bent down close to her ear. "You are a selfish bitch. After all I did for you, this is how you repay me. You better wake the fuck up or I will kill you myself," he growled in her ear as if his words would bring her into consciousness.

Jordan's words were interrupted by a small knock on the door. Diamond entered, looking different but well. The last time Jordan had had real contact with her, she was a half-dressed, gaunt skeleton on her knees begging him for mercy. Right then, Jordan remembered how powerful he had felt when he had left a bruised and battered Diamond lying in a putrid heap of her own body fluids.

Diamond was now dressed conservatively in an A-line pencil skirt, a neat ruffle-front blouse and classy pumps. She wore limited makeup, which showed off more of her natural beauty and strong features. When he met her, Jordan remembered thinking that Diamond was as pretty as Halle Berry, only a few shades darker and a little more rugged. Now that she wasn't scantily clad and wearing gaudy makeup, Jordan thought she looked not only respectable but beautiful. Jordan had been keeping tabs on her over the past year. It wasn't that hard to track down her phone number, especially because she was married to one of the most popular pastors in New York.

Neither Jordan nor Dominique uttered a word to one another. He didn't know whether to call her Diamond or Dominique.

Dominique stared at Casey, her feet seemingly rooted to the floor. Tubes emanated from various parts of Casey's body. Diamond could count at least seven. The last time Dominique had witnessed a sight like this was when Mama Grady was on her deathbed in the hospital. The pungent smell of disinfectant made Dominique want to hurl. A thin sheen of sweat began to form on her forehead and over her lip. A small tornado of memories began to whip up in Dominique's mind. It was the past that propelled her forward to Casey's side.

Chapter Two

Coming of Age

Brooklyn, New York

Dominique's throat was raw from screaming. She opened her mouth again, but no sound came out. Rocking back and forth, she continued to cradle her mother's head. She wanted to cry, but she had exhausted the energy necessary to produce tears.

Dominique's mother's eyes were open and glassy. Her hair, damp with sweat, was matted to Dominique's thigh. Dominique felt as though huge needles were pricking her legs. Even if she could move, she refused to do so.

She wasn't sure what time the ambulance finally arrived. She certainly didn't remember the paramedics peeling her away from her mother's body, like a drowning victim in the middle of the sea clinging to a floating piece of driftwood. Dominique could barely remember the ride to the hospital, except for the EMT's words: "It appears the patient is in cardiac arrest." She remembered shouts over shortwave radios and frantic calls for additional tubes, needles and bags of fluid.

The squeal of the ambulance did not bother Dominique as much as the bumpy ride. Watching her mother on the stretcher, limp and jerky, unable to brace herself against the turbulence made a pain shoot through Dominique's chest. Her mother was usually able to stand up against anything.

Dominique was ushered out of the ambulance and placed in a crowded waiting area while her mother, now plugged with tubes, was rushed through two large silver doors that only allowed entry with a swipe card. Her mother disappeared among a throng of white coats and scrubs.

Dominique was alone. The last time she remembered being in a hospital was when she busted her chin in gymnastics class and needed stitches.

Dominique sat quietly as people hustled past her. Every now and then someone in the waiting room would jump up and yell profanities to the triage nurse who sat behind the thick, scratched-up plexiglass. The waiting room chairs were a dirty, hard orange, yellow and blue. In one corner, a man resembling a coal miner, with black soot covering his face and hands, sat talking to himself and clutching to his chest several plastic bags filled with recyclable bottles. A few seats away from him sat a girl no older than Dominique, holding to the mouth of a small baby a tube connected to a nebulizer. Dominique's mother had always opted out of seeking treatment at this hospital, claiming "we can afford better than the county." Now she realized why her mother had been so insistent about looking elsewhere.

It felt like a lifetime before a tall lady with salt-and-pepper bangs and a fake black ponytail approached Dominique. "Hi, my name is Cathy. I'm a social worker," the woman said softly, extending her hand toward Dominique. She ignored the woman's hand, and was barely able to stretch her sore, red-rimmed eyes to look up at the woman.

"Dominique, honey, I know this is difficult," the woman consoled, sitting down in a hard, plastic chair.

What the hell did this woman know about it being hard? Was her mother dead? Was she left with no mother and no father? Dominique wanted to shout all these questions, but instead she remained silent. She was old enough to know that she was not going to be able to go back home alone. Her grandmother had died the year before and there was only one other person left to take her in. The social worker asked a series of questions, assuring her that she would "find the right person" to care for her. It had taken Dominique a few tries before she remembered her grandmother's old phone number, since she hadn't dialed it in over a year. Dominique knew that her mother's sister still resided in her grandmother's old apartment. Her aunt was probably her only hope for staying out of the foster care system.

Several hours passed and Dominique began to doze in the waiting room. Every now and then, the doctor or social worker would check on her and whisper in earnest. Dominique had counted a total of six "code blues" over the hospital loud speakers since she'd arrived. That's what they'd called her mother on the ride over. She wondered if six other girls had lost the only person in the world they had left.

"Where is my damn niece?" a voice barked, followed by the click-clack of high heels. Dominique recognized the voice immediately. It was her aunt, Awilda. Dominique hadn't seen her aunt since her grandmother's funeral and the catfight that had ensued between Awilda and her mother following the service. She remembered Awilda calling her mother a "stuck-up, wannabe bitch" and her mother calling her aunt "a no-good, classless whore."

"My sister is dead and y'all got this goddamn baby sittin' in these hard-ass chairs? What happened to the comfortable kind y'all give the white people when they grievin'?" Awilda hollered to no one in particular, switching her hips down the quiet hospital corridor.

Crass, Dominique thought. That was the word her mother had used when referring to her aunt.

"Oh, there you are, baby," Awilda moaned, softening her voice and extending her arms well before she reached Dominique. Bending down for a hug, Awilda grabbed Dominique's head and forced it into her chest in a rough display of familial affection. Dominique felt suffocated by her aunt's bulging cleavage and cheap Jean Naté perfume. She smelled like a cross between a tree-shaped car air freshener and a can of Lysol.

"Ahem." Dominique let out a small cough as she tried to disengage herself from the all-consuming embrace.

"I ain't gonna let nothin' happen to you. It's okay, it's okay," Awilda continued, stroking Dominique's head like she was a small dog.

Dominique scrunched up her face and pulled away. She wasn't crying and didn't need to be comforted. Folding her arms in front of her chest, she gave Awilda a once-over. *Too much makeup, too much perfume, clothes are too small, fake hair, fake nails, and smells like cigarettes.*

Her aunt had never been nice to Dominique as a child. In fact, she vividly remembered Awilda cornering her at her grandmother's house, pointing a long, black-painted fingernail in her face and saying, "Your mother raising you to be a *bogee* bitch, just like her. Well, I tell you what. You ain't no better than ya aunty. You never know, one day you might have to sell your fuckin' soul to the devil too."

Cathy, the social worker, had asked Awilda to step away from Dominique so that she and Awilda could talk. Dominique knew they were talking about her and her mother. After they were done conferring on Dominique's fate, the social worker bent down to reach eye level with Dominique. "Dominique, honey. Your aunty here is going to care of you tonight. I will be sending someone to her home to make sure it is fit for you," Cathy started.

At that, Awilda threw up her hands and interrupted. "Look. I've known this here baby all of her life. I'm her next of kin and you don't need to survey shit at my house," Awilda spoke indignantly.

Cathy stared Awilda down before she replied, "It's our protocol, *ma'am*." With a sigh, Cathy gazed at Dominique with a look of sympathy, as if to apologize for releasing her into Awilda's custody.

"It was all a dream/ I used to read *Word Up* Magazine/ Salt n' Pepa and Heavy D up in the limousine . . ." Outside of the hospital emergency entrance, a black Lexus Coupe sat blaring Biggie Smalls, the bass loud enough to shake the concrete. "C'mon, that's our ride," Awilda said, rushing toward the vehicle.

Dominique walked slowly to the car, thinking that it looked like the typical drug dealer car her mother always pointed out when they went to visit her grandmother's neighborhood. Her mother repeatedly warned her to also "stay away from boys who drive those kinds of cars."

"What the hell is your problem, little girl? Why are you standing here like you seen a ghost?" Awilda, asked grabbing Dominique's arm to pull her along.

"I'm coming!" Dominique shouted, yanking her arm away. She wanted to scream and cry right there. Images of her mother's face still clouded her mind.

"Well, come the hell on then! I know ya mama just died but I need to get back home!" Awilda grumbled, focusing her attention back on the vehicle.

Once inside, Dominique folded her arms across her chest and told herself she wouldn't say a word to her aunt or the man driving. Awilda leaned over and gave the driver a kiss on the cheek. He wore dark shades and never even said hello to them. Awilda reached down and turned up the music, thinking Dominique couldn't hear her conversation.

"Wassup, baby? Sorry to call you out so late but my sister just died. They said it was that bitch's heart. Same shit that killed my mother. Maybe if she wasn't such a stuck-up bitch that fucking heart would've kept on working," Awilda spat as she lit up a cigarette. Dominique hated cigarettes, but she despised her aunt. "One good thing about it, that bitch of a sister of mine always worked which means a social security check for her little spoiled ass brat back there. Ching, ching! I could use some extra cash!" Awilda continued blowing smoke rings and laughing wickedly.

"That money runs out at eighteen. You better put that ass to work before that," the man said, seeming to finally find his voice.

Dominique bit the inside of her cheek to keep herself from crying out.

Arriving at her new home, Dominique looked up at the sign: LOUIS H. PINK HOUSES, it read. Her mother had told her that Awilda still lived in the projects, but Dominique had never been to Awilda's house. She had always encountered her aunt at her grandmother's new place. The building they pulled up to was lively. There were children running and playing; music blasting; and some older women sitting out on the benches. They had an entire spread of food on a little table, like they were having a party.

"C'mon, get out and stop acting like you ain't never see your own kind before," Awilda said to Dominique, referring to the fact that Dominique and her mother lived in Park Slope with mostly white people. Dominique climbed out of the car and followed Awilda into the building. Dominique immediately cupped her hand over her nose. The smell of urine hit her nostrils with potency. This new life would take some getting used to for sure.

Hildale, Utah

Casey jumped at the sound of loud knocks on the door. "I . . . I'm using the toilet," she stuttered, looking down at her soiled underwear.

"Casey, we don't lock doors around here, now open up!" Jocintha, her sister yelled from the other side.

"Hold on, I'm coming," Casey stammered nervously, folding her undergarments and dress into a tight wad. Looking around the nearly empty bathroom, Casey frantically searched for a place to hide her soiled garments. She knew if anyone found out about her new "problem" she'd immediately be sent to the "prophet" for marriage. Casey had seen it happen to her four older sisters. As soon as they became "women," they were added to the prophets' dream book and scheduled for marriage, most of the time to much older men—men who also happened to be uncles or cousins. Casey had overheard that as soon as she became a woman, she was going to be given to Samson Jeffers, a fat, ugly first cousin of Casey's biological mother. Samson already had four wives; the last one was just fourteen years old.

Casey didn't want to get married. At thirteen-and-a-half, she dreamt of leaving Backwater Creek to live a different life. Casey wanted to be a ballerina, just like she'd seen in the magazines that she stole from the supermarket on the few occasions her mother went to the "non-believers" store to pick up some necessities. Casey would head straight for the magazine racks when her mother wasn't looking. She had pictures stashed under her mattress of the Juilliard School in

New York City. Casey told herself that as soon as she was old enough, she would leave the compound and go to Juilliard to become a world renowned ballerina. She believed that as soon as the administrators at the school saw her beauty and grace, they would accept her right away.

"What's going on here?" Casey heard the voice of Marianne, one of her father's five wives.

"Casey has gone and locked the door. I don't know what she's doing in there," Jocintha answered, being her usual snitch self.

"Casey?" Marianne called out, twisting the doorknob back and forth several times.

"I'm coming," Casey announced, her voice quivering. Casey quickly stuffed the balled-up clothing into the toilet bowl tank, making a mental note to dispose of it as soon as she got the chance. Rushing over to the door, Casey flung it open and pushed passed Jocintha and Marianne, making a dash for her bedroom. *Maybe they'll be able to tell if they look at my face,* Casey thought as she kept her head down.

"That is the strangest little girl I know," Marianne mumbled, rushing into the bathroom to inspect it. Jocintha ran behind Casey. They were the same age. Casey's mother gave birth to her in August of 1983, and Jocintha's mother delivered in September of the same year. The two sister wives often joked about how they must've gotten pregnant a week apart, on their assigned nights to spend with Casey's father—Warren Jessop Pete, assistant to the prophet of the Fundamentalist Church of Latter Day Saints (FLDS).

That night Casey tossed and turned with cramps. She feared that if she asked her mother for relief her father would find out about her condition. But living in a house filled with women—five mothers and twelve sisters—it was simply a matter of time. When her mother found out, she gave Casey homemade Maxi pads fashioned out of gauze and terry cloth, and told her she was a woman now. Casey would be expected to quit school to work on the compound.

It was only a week after she had got her period that Casey's mother entered her room with a small picnic basket and a warm smile.

"Casey, honey, it's time for us to have the talk," her mother said. Casey stashed her ballerina pictures and followed her mother outside. They walked along the compound toward the area where all of their special occasions were held. Casey had been there many times in her life, for weddings, baptisms, funerals, and family fun events. It was also where the prophet laid down the law. All of the compound residents had just gathered there the week before to watch Casey's friend Nicole get whipped for kissing a boy before she was married. The prophet had whipped Nicole until she bled through her dress. Casey's mother had whispered to her, "Now no one will marry that girl."

Backwater Creek had about one hundred small, wood-frame homes, most with no running water or toilets. The red dirt that covered most of the compound gave the entire place a reddish glow, and if she stood on the roof of her house she could see the Moccassin Mountains Range. It was completely cut off from the outside world and the male residents took turns standing security guard at the front gates. People of the outside world were referred to as "foreigners."

Casey felt ashamed by the stares she received as she walked along the dirt roads of Backwater Creek with her mother. Each time she passed one of the run-down plywood houses, residents would stop and stare. Everyone knew that she was a woman now. It didn't take long for news to spread. Casey tugged at her long sleeves, making sure no one could see her skin. Women on the compound wore long sleeve dresses with long skirts that came past their feet. Most of them wore the same hair styles as well—a large flipped bang and a single long braid down the back. Most little girls would be so proud once their hair grew long enough to style it like the other FLDS women.

Casey and her mother finally arrived at the occasion area. Nicole's blood still stained the dirt. Casey swallowed hard and used her boot to cover the old blood in the dirt. Casey's sister AmberRae had received "the talk" shortly before she was married off to Clayton Grant—their father's half brother.

Casey's mother smiled and asked her to sit down on the knitted blanket they'd made together the year before. Everything they wore and used was either handmade or homegrown. "Casey, the prophet has added your name to the dream book. Your betrothal has been arranged," her mother announced in her soft, cottony voice. Casey lowered her head. "Your father's place in heaven is dependent on you now, honey," her mother continued, touching her golden hair gently.

"I don't want to get married. Can't father make it into heaven any other way?" Casey asked, her voice cracking.

Her mother opened her arms for a hug. "No, honey. The prophet has spoken and given your father his orders. You will be married. It is time," her mother said with finality.

Casey sobbed in to her mother's chest. "Please, mother, please!" Casey cried. Her mother just remained silent, stroking her hair. Although Casey had been born right in Backwater Creek, her mother had not. Casey's older brother, Ethan, had told her that their mother had been born into what he'd termed a "normal family." It was not until she met and fell in love with their father that she'd joined FLDS and decided to live the polygamist life style. Her mother, however, was not their father's first wife or last. Ethan told Casey many stories of how Rebecca, the senior wife, had abused their mother and the children. According to Ethan, after her mother complained to the prophet about Rebecca, the prophet spent thirty-nights with their mother and then reassigned Rebecca to another husband. When Casey discovered that her mother had given up a normal life of choices and freedom to live on the compound as a polygamist and follow the prophet's every order, she believed her mother to be an essentially weak person. This had always made Casey feel sorry for her mother. But over the years, the sorrow turned into frustration, anger and resentment.

Harlem, New York

"Ahh!" Jordan jerked awake. Inhaling deeply, he quickly tried to catch some air. He felt like he was drowning. He was out of the bed in one leap, chest heaving. "What the fuck?" he screamed, wiping the dampness from his face. At first he thought he was having a nightmare, but his wet wifebeater and underwear told him otherwise.

"Yeah, muthafucka, I threw water in your face. You see the goddamn time? Ain't nobody sleeping all day up in my fuckin' house. A shiftless niggah, that's what you turned out to be. Now get ya black ass up and find a fuckin' job," his mother screamed, threatening to upend the bucket of ice-cold water she held tightly in her hands.

Jordan bit down into his jaw and clenched his fists at his side. He rocked on his heels, willing himself not to hit the woman who had given birth to him. That's all she was to him: his birth canal, a way into this fucked-up world.

"I raised three sons and you the only black bastard who

ain't amount to shit. I should've known when I laid down with ya dog-ass father I'd wake the fuck up with a black-ass flea like you!" she screamed, hitting the bottom of the bucket for emphasis. "I broke my back to put ya ass through school and this is what the fuck you do with a degree? Hmph, you not livin' in here. Look at Ethan, a real estate mogul. Ain't even get to go to college and made somethin' outta himself. And look at David . . ." the vituperative words continued to roll off her tongue. Before she could finish her degrading rant, Jordan sucked in his bottom lip, yanked off his wet wifebeater and grabbed a dry sweat shirt and a pair of jeans. He pushed past his mother, whose veins were now clearly visible and pounding in her high yellow neck.

"Go on! You better not come back up in here another day without some money or a fuckin' job!" she screamed at his back as he walked out the front door of their brownstone.

Jordan stumbled down the front stoop stairs and onto the sidewalk. Tears burned at the backs of his eyes as he walked dejectedly down the street. He had no idea where he was headed, but wherever it was, he was sure it was going to be a paper chase. He was going to show that bitch of a mother of his. Once he made it, he'd take his money, wipe his ass with it, and throw it in her face.

He hated his mother. For as long as he could remember she never had a kind word for him. Jordan was the youngest of Trina King's three sons and the one she resented the most. Trina had been married to the father of her children until Jordan came along. After taking one look at Jordan's dark skin, Ethan Sr. had told Trina the boy wasn't his. Ethan Sr. had heard rumors that while he was out hustling up enough money to feed Trina and the kids, she had been sleeping with his archenemy.

When Ethan left her, Trina struggled, and she took out

every bit of her frustration on Jordan. Once, when he was five, she had beat all of the skin off his back because he had spilled milk trying to get a bowl of cereal for himself. She called Jordan degrading names on a daily basis. She also turned her other sons against Jordan, making them believe the reason they were without their father was because of their little bastard brother. Jordan's two other brothers often beat on him at whim and called him names with no repercussions from their mother.

The one thing Trina could not deny was that Jordan was her most book-smart child. Jordan excelled in school and he was the only one of her three boys to finish high school. When Jordan enrolled at Hunter College as a business major, Trina took all of the credit. She often ranted and raved about paying for him to go to school, when in actuality all she'd done was provide Jordan with carfare; state and federal government grants—TAP and PELL—had really paid for his schooling. Jordan had just graduated and was trying to find a job, but his mother didn't want to hear it. Each time he landed a position, he would inevitably get into a dust-up with his supervisor. Jordan had trouble controlling his anger and he definitely could not deal very well with authority.

"Dayum, young blood, who done pissed in your Cheerios?" a voice called out from a big-body Mercedes-Benz S500 that pulled up as Jordan almost reached the corner of his block. The driver was flashing a diamond-studded smile. He was the one person Jordan had tried to avoid since he was a kid. But today, Jordan stopped and smiled back.

"Where you headed, young blood? You look like you need a friend," the driver said. It was C-Lo. Everybody in Harlem knew who C-Lo was, especially Jordan. C-Lo was the hood's jack-of-all-trades. He was a well-known pimp and notorious drug dealer around Harlem. C-Lo had a reputation that preceded him. When he came around or stepped into a room, everyone knew who he was and what he was capable of. C-Lo had been trying to recruit Jordan for years, but Jordan had chosen to go to college and try to make his money legitimately.

As a child, Jordan didn't revere C-Lo like all of the other kids in the neighborhood. He was not impressed that C-Lo had a new pair of kicks for every day of the week or that he wore the biggest gold rope chains and rings on every finger. In fact, Jordan hated C-Lo and he had good reason. Jordan often wondered if his mother knew that he'd seen C-Lo leaving her bedroom many nights after the sounds of them fucking had awoken him. It was a pattern that Jordan had become accustomed to. First his mother would complain about being broke. She would curse and call Jordan a black piece of shit and say he wouldn't amount to anything. Then she would smoke a few cigarettes, make a phone call, and later on that night Jordan would see C-Lo creeping in his house when his mother thought he was asleep. The next day, his mother would have a fistful of cash to spend.

C-Lo had plenty of money and Jordan needed it. Putting his feelings of hatred aside, he walked toward the car and climbed in.

"How you doin', college boy? Them college degrees ain't done shit for you, huh? You ready to finally take me up on my offer?" C-Lo smiled, the diamonds on his fronts sparkling like stars in a nighttime sky.

"Yeah, I'm ready," Jordan replied in an almost inaudible whisper.

"I thought you'd come around one day. How's your mother doing?" C-Lo asked, snickering. Jordan bit into his jaw and looked out the car window as they drove away from his house.

Chapter Three

The Lesser of Two Evils

"Jordan, what did you do?" Dominique screamed, placing her hand over her mouth as she looked down at the bloody mess.

"Oh my God! " Casey screamed, jumping up and down in a panic.

"Everybody just shut the fuck up and calm down!" Jordan barked, pacing the floor. He took a long sip of Mylanta and continued to pace.

Dominique was haunted by thoughts from her past as she sped home from seeing Casey in the hospital. The sight of Casey had brought back memories Dominique had worked hard to suppress. The story Jordan had given her about what had happened to Casey didn't add up. Knowing what Jordan was capable of, Casey's "attempted suicide" just didn't sound right.

Dominique finally made it home. Fumbling through her pocketbook for her keys, Dominique looked around nervously. Alton's car was missing from the driveway, which was a good sign. Letting out a deep sigh, she finally located her keys, peering over her shoulder once more before she rushed through the front door.

A bolt of lightning flashed behind Dominique's eyes. With a scream stuck in the back of her throat, a brutal force pulled her down on the hardwood floor of the foyer. The sudden motion caused her pocketbook strap to twist, making a tourniquet on her arm, cutting off the circulation. She could hear his animalistic breathing.

Another blow caused an unbearable pain in her head. "Ahhhhhhhh!" She was finally able to let out a blood-curdling scream. Instinctively, Dominique placed her hands up in defense, but to no avail. Another blow to the top of her head caused the images from her past to appear again. Dominique saw herself stumbling backward. She watched Jordon's foot connect with the center of her face. She felt the bone between her eyes crack. "J . . . Alton, no!" Dominique finally managed to scream, catching her words before the wrong name slipped from her lips. The scenes were so similar—the past and the present were blending into one.

"You are the most disobedient woman alive!" Alton growled as he wrapped his gorilla hands around her ponytail. Dominique let her body go limp. She knew the results of fighting against Alton. "Where have you been?" he screamed, reaching under her bowed head and slamming his balled fist into the same spot that Jordon had injured years earlier. Blood sprayed from Dominique's face onto Alton's pants like a lawn sprinkler. As he yanked her head back to look into her eyes, blood from her nose dripped into the back of her throat, threatening to choke her.

"Alton, pa-lease!" she gasped out, pleading as he dragged her across the floor. She could feel the skin on her knees splitting. An open-handed slap landed on her cheek. Dominique saw small squirming flashes of light out of the side of her eyes. Now she knew what people meant when they said they saw "stars." She prayed Alton wouldn't kick her this time. Dominique was sure her ribs hadn't fully healed from the last time. Another blow would surely send bone fragments into her heart or

lungs and kill her instantly. The pain pulsing through her
head became unbearable. She placed her hands on top of
Alton's, trying to pry his fingers from her scalp.

"You need to repent today! For God says the husband is
the head of his wife! She must obey and be humble!" Alton
roared, continuing his assault.

Dominique knew that he would beat her until the demon
that she was sure lived inside of him had finally had enough.
Then he would reach down to the crumpled pile that was
his wife and help her up off the floor. He would force
her to have Bible Study, followed by sex. As he dragged her
up the staircase, Alton punched her in the back, causing her
to involuntarily emit a loud cough. He'd literally knocked
the wind out of her. Urine ran down her legs. As she drifted
to a place between consciousness and hell, she thought about
Casey, lying with tubes coming out of her body, close to death.
At this moment, Dominique would have gladly changed places
with Casey.

When Alton had finished "God's work," he threw her limp,
injured arm around his neck and carried her like a wounded
comrade in a war. "I'm sorry.

I just love you and the Lord so much," he whispered as
he placed Dominique gently on the floor of the bathroom.
Dominique struggled to breathe. She felt like all of her ribs
were broken. Her knees burned from the friction burns she
had suffered while being dragged. As bad as she wanted to
scream out or even moan, Dominique did not want to take a
chance on making him angry again.

"Come here, let me help you clean up," Alton consoled
in a low, soft voice that was completely different than the
booming, maniacal voice he'd been using just a few minutes
earlier. Dominique struggled to open her eyes. Blood and
tears had dried and crusted around them, nearly sealing them

shut. She lay in the fetal position in a growing pool of blood, every inch of her body on fire.

Alton went into the linen closet and got a hand towel. Dominique could hear the water running. Then she felt the warm rag against her battered skin. "Ssss," she winced, shrinking away from his touch.

"I am so sorry," he said, wiping more blood from her face and neck.

"I know you are. I forgive you," Dominique whispered, knowing it was what he wanted to hear.

Brice looked at his new gold badge again. He breathed on it, rubbing it on his shirt to get it to shine. He liked the sound of his new title, "Detective Brice Simpson." Placing his belt badge back on his Armani suit pants, he stretched his arms out and looked around the bustling detective squad room of the Brooklyn North Task Force. He tapped his fingers on his new desk, albeit old and rickety. He had finally made it. As a patrol cop, the only thing he had was a tiny steel locker sandwiched between slews of other lockers in his precinct. But street patrols and uniforms were a thing of the past.

Brice looked around the room at the wanted posters. Being only twenty-eight years old and from Brooklyn, he recognized more than a few faces on the posters. He probably knew where to find the suspects, too.

"Hey, Simpson, you think the good commissioner promoted you to sit there and look at the manicure Kim Ling gave you?" Detective Sergeant Curruthers yelled out as he walked toward Brice, his joke garnering snickers from the rest of the squad. Brice felt his cheeks flame.

"Here you go, some work. I know you're not used to it, but up here we work," Sergeant Curruthers said, slamming a stack of case files on Brice's desk.

"I ain't never scared," Brice said jokingly, letting out a short, nervous chuckle. Looking down at the files he saw a big red sticker labeled, COLD CASE FILES.

"Aww, shit," he cursed, flipping through the stack. He looked up and saw that the other detectives were staring and laughing at him.

"The new guy gets the dogs . . . you know, the shit nobody else wants. We don't care how much cops and robbers you played as a street cop, solve those sons of bitches and you really earn this promotion," Sergeant Curruthers said utterly serious for a change, popping his suspenders that looked stretched to the limit over his huge gut.

Brice had been a New York City Police Department patrol cop for six years before he shot two fleeing armed robbery suspects who had turned their weapons on Brice's partner, wounding him in the stomach. Brice had been lauded by the NYPD for his heroic and courageous actions and earned a promotion to detective as a result. What the Department didn't know was that, yes, Brice had given chase and drawn his weapon, but the only reason he hadn't also been shot was because one of the robbers had been Brice's childhood best friend, Earl.

Brice could still hear Earl's words. "Wait, niggah, don't shoot. Wait the fuck a minute! B-boy? You a fuckin' cop?" Earl had asked, calling Brice by his childhood tag name. Earl was clearly shocked to see his best friend in the graveee blues, which is what they called the navy blue NYPD uniforms on the streets, making reference to how many black boys the NYPD had put in the grave.

Brice had ignored his old friend's question, but kept his gun trained on Earl.

They locked eyes. Their past indiscretions stood between them like a giant ogre, scary and threatening to eat them alive.

"A'ight, B-boy, I'ma drop my weapon," Earl said, calmly placing one hand up and preparing to bend down to drop his weapon.

"Fuck that!" Earl's accomplice screamed out, raising his gun. With that distraction and without thinking first, Brice opened fire on both of them. He watched Earl fold to the ground like a deflated balloon.

"Damn, B-boy . . . you was my brother from another mother," Earl rasped before throngs of police officers descended upon the scene in response to the 10-13 that Brice had previously called over the radio. Brice found out a few hours later that he had "heroically" taken the suspects down. The entire scene had taken a toll on him and he still suffered nightmares. He had not planned for Earl to find out his secret like that. Brice was determined to take his promotion to detective and fuck the wheels off of it to move up the ranks. The further removed he was from the streets, the easier it would be to live with the choice he'd made during the robbery.

Brice flipped through several of the cold case files. Many of the cases were related to indigent people found dead under bridges and in abandoned buildings; some were of known gang members found dead in project elevators and stairwells; and others of dead crackheads. But one case stood out from all the rest. A fourteen-year-old girl had been found bludgeoned to death in a Dumpster behind a Brooklyn bodega. Brice immediately thought of his little sister, Ciara, who'd just turned sixteen. He was Ciara's big brother, but acted more in the capacity of her father. He had stepped in where his alcoholic stepfather had stepped out. Overprotective big brother was an understatement.

Brice opened the folder and on the inside cover were several crime scene photographs. Brice winced, feeling the pain the girl must have endured. He could hardly make out the girl's face in the pictures. Her head, from the neck up, resembled a blob—a red clump of flesh with no definition. Brice couldn't distinguish her eyes or nose. Her hair was matted with blood. Whoever murdered her left her butt naked. She'd been beaten all over her body and then dumped atop bags of trash, an indistinguishable mass of flesh and blood. Bugs had already started eating away at the flesh by the time the pictures were taken.

Brice shuffled the photos and looked at the girl after she had been cleaned up by the medical examiner. Although her face was completely disfigured, like someone with elephantitis, Brice could tell that she was just a baby. Her breasts were barely developed, her fingers small and slender like delicate straws. The medical examiner had ruled the cause of death as a brain hemorrhage. *Who would beat such a young girl so unmercifully?* Brice's fingers closed tightly around the file. He meticulously reviewed each piece of paper and flipped through all the notes. A handwritten Post-it note had been left in the file, where someone had scribbled: "Runaway prostitute got herself killed. Case closed."

Brice squinted his eyes into little slits and feverishly turned the pages to find out which detective had been assigned the case. "D'Guilio," he mumbled under his breath. "It fucking figures . . . white prick. If she were a white runaway, would he have come to the same conclusion?" It was apparent that the detective assigned the case didn't bother to fully investigate before having it deemed a cold case.

Brice glanced at the address where the body was found. He grabbed his gun out of his desk drawer and put it in his shoulder holster. "I'll be back!" he yelled to no one in particular.

***

Jordan was asleep on a small foldout hospital chair/bed. The nurse came in to check on Casey's vitals before the shift change. Jordan was awakened by her movement. "How she doin'?" he asked, clearing his throat.

The nurse didn't turn to acknowledge him; instead she continued her work. "As good as can be expected for what she ingested. Lucky to be alive," the nurse said dryly. Everyone in the hospital now knew who Casey and Jordan were, thanks to the small media and porno paparazzi that had gathered outside. When the nurse left, Jordan slumped down in the chair. He looked over at Casey's stiff form and started thinking of his plan B. Jordan always kept a plan B. He had promised himself he would never go back to being broke. Women were the key to his success and fortune in the porn industry. Jordan picked up his cell phone and scrolled through his contacts. Finding the number he wanted, he looked over at Casey, shrugged his shoulders and left the room.

"Wassup, ma?" Jordan said into the phone when the line picked up. "Can I see you tonight?" he asked. "A'ight, I'll pick you up right where I met you. Be as sexy as you were that day," Jordan said, laying his game down. Jordan hadn't had a stable of working girls in a minute, but he knew that his skills were there, even if they'd been lying dormant for some time. Shit, if he could do it then, he damn sure could do it now.

Chapter Four

Innocence Lost

<u>*Brooklyn, New York*</u>

Awilda pulled back the comforter and slapped Dominique's bare legs.

"Mmmm," Dominique moaned, snatching a corner of the blanket to pull over her head.

"You know the deal, so get ya ass up," Awilda said, yanking the entire comforter off Dominique's body and flinging it across the room.

"Whatchu doin'?" Dominique hollered, her mind still fuzzy with sleep. It had been a long night for Dominique. The throbbing between her legs was proof. *What the fuck does this bitch want from me?* Throwing her shapely legs over the side of the bed, Dominique stumbled out of bed.

"Get the fuck up and wash ya stank ass fish box and let's go. Time is money," Awilda spat, marching out of the living room, which also doubled as Dominique's bedroom. Dominique padded into the bathroom and slammed the door so hard the roaches began to scatter.

"I hate this bitch. I gotta get the fuck up outta here," Dominique cursed as she began washing up with the little chips of soap that were left. "All this fuckin' for money and this bitch don't even buy fuckin' soap," Dominique cursed. She had developed a potty mouth and an attitude to match. She was not the same little girl Awilda had taken home from the hospital when her mother had died. Dominique had been in Awilda's house for three years and shit just got worse and worse each year. When she first arrived, the worst thing Awilda made her do was clean up all of the time. Then she graduated to making Dominique serve her men friends drinks and food when they came over. Awilda was never satisfied with anything Dominique did for her. Then, in Dominique's assessment, Awilda lost her fucking mind, when her greed for money made her stoop to a new low.

The first time Awilda made Dominique attend one of her "meetings," Dominique had just turned fourteen. They'd gotten into a black Cadillac with two older men. The thick marijuana smoke assailed her nose and cast a thick, grey haze inside the car. The man in the passenger seat looked back at Dominique and smiled.

"I like 'em young and fresh just like that," he said.

"Well, I don't like them old and nasty," Dominique responded with sass.

Awilda let out a nervous laugh, then leaned in to Dominique's side. "Shut the fuck up or your ass will be on the streets." Awilda gritted her teeth, her breath hot on Dominique's ear.

When they arrived at the Galaxy Motel on Pennsylvania Avenue, Awilda pulled Dominique aside and handed her a silver-wrapped Trojan condom. "What's this for?" Dominique asked, her eyes wide with surprise. She was fourteen and had never seen a condom, although she'd heard about them from the sexually active kids in her school.

"Make sure that muthafucka puts it on. I will be right next door so knock on the wall if he doesn't," Awilda whispered, like she was giving Dominique some good motherly advice.

"What are you talking about? I ain't about to have sex with that old man. I'm a virgin," Dominique replied, furrowing her eyebrows as her voice began to quiver. *This bitch has finally lost her mind!*

"Oh, you will do whatever he asks you to do. And if he asks you to fuck him . . . you will. That's the name of the game, little girl. I been taking care of you for a year and your ass ain't cheap to feed and clothe," Awilda retorted, lighting the tip of her cigarette, her hands trembling. "Now, be fucking quiet before somebody in here thinks something funny," Awilda instructed, looking around the lobby nervously. Awilda's demeanor told Dominique that her aunt knew better. She knew damn well a little girl shouldn't be in a nasty-ass, short-stay motel being forced to sell herself.

Dominique looked around the lobby. There wasn't a damn soul in the filthy-ass lobby who looked as if they had one piece of moral fiber. The front desk manager looked like a straight crackhead and there were several people hanging out. A man leaned near the elevator doors in a steady nod. He'd nod so far over he looked like he'd hit the floor. When he was seconds from hitting the floor, he'd pop back up, scratch his nose, look around and start his nod process again. None of these degenerates looked willing or capable of coming to her rescue.

Dominique spotted two girls who looked to be about her age, huddled together looking out of the glass lobby doors like they were expecting someone. They were dressed just like Dominique had seen Awilda dress on many occasions. One wore a pink corset top and black lace panties to cover her bottom; the other wore a red lace negligee, fishnet stockings and stilettos. Both had on bright-colored wigs, which gave the illusion that they were older. But Dominique knew they couldn't have been much older than herself. Looking down at her jeans and hoodie outfit, Dominique felt sorry for the other girls. She didn't even realize she wasn't much better off than they were.

"A'ight ladies," the Cadillac driver said, cracking a yellow-toothed grin as he held up the battered key ring for the room. Dominique tried to be strong, but a choked sob escaped anyway.

"Awww, what the fuck is this shit? I ain't about to deal with no baby cry bullshit," the paying customer grumbled.

"Look, she is just a little nervous. You said you wanted fresh meat, right? So just bear with her," Awilda placated, gripping Dominique's arm tightly so she wouldn't run. Awilda had already been promised extra cash for her young niece. "I'll come in the room for a minute to help her get comfortable," Awilda continued, trying to console the old pervert.

"Whatchu talkin', gal?" the driver interjected. He wanted Awilda to himself.

"I'll make it up to you, baby. You can watch and then we will get our groove on," Awilda said to the driver, who was clearly going to be her john for the night.

Once inside the room, Awilda pulled Dominique in to the bathroom. She was crying so hard she could barely see where she was walking.

"Shut the fuck up! You wanna have some place to live, right? This is what you need to do to survive. Forget about the fucking life you used to live. Your mother wanted you to think you was too good to live like this . . . well, you ain't! Now shut the fuck up and take off your fuckin' clothes. You ain't got no choice. I'm all you got!" Awilda hissed, a scowl on her face. Dominique could've sworn she saw red fire in Awilda's eyes.

Awilda opened the bathroom door as Dominique slowly

removed her clothes, her body trembling. "Here she come, baby," Awilda sang, like she was introducing Dominique at a grade school pageant.

Dominique used the tops of her arms to cover her small breasts and crossed her hands in front of her pubic area. She walked slowly over to the bed, barely able to breathe between sobs. The fat, hairy, old man was fondling his little shriveled dick, while he waited patiently for his prize. Dominique looked down at all of the hair that covered his chest, stomach and legs and she wanted to vomit.

"Put that condom on, baby," Awilda said to the man, as she prevented Dominique from going any further until the man did as he was told. For a minute Awilda tried to seem responsible.

"Lay on the bed," Awilda then instructed Dominique.

Dominique closed her eyes and did as she was told. The man immediately attempted to mount her, forcing himself between her partially opened legs.

"This girl gotta open her legs wider! Shit, I'm a man, not a boy!" he screamed to Awilda, the smell of Blackberry Brandy escaped from his chapped bubble lips and shot up Dominique's nostrils so fast she could taste the sweet liquor in the back of her throat.

"Okay . . . okay, let me just help her relax," Awilda placated, rubbing his nasty, hairy stomach. The other man stood in a corner and rubbed himself, aroused from watching.

"C'mon, Dominique, he ain't got all day and neither do I," Awilda said with clenched teeth, digging her inch-long, round-tip nails into Dominique's thighs.

"Owww!" Dominique shrieked as Awilda released her dented flesh and propped her legs open. The man let out a pleased snort as he forced his slimy tool into Dominique's virginal opening. Dominique let out a grating cry, something half-human, half-animal.

"Yeah, this some good shit here," the man grunted as he picked up speed. Dominique felt like she would pass out. "It burns!!" she yelled in agony. It felt like someone had lit a torch between her legs; the burning was unbearable. Dominique's legs trembled from the pain.

"Yeah, oh yeah," the man grunted, grinding into her body as far as he could go. Awilda stood up, watching, taking a long drag on her cigarette until her work was done.

Awilda pounded on the bathroom door. "Come the fuck on, Dominique! Don't let me have to call you again."

The memories always fucked with Dominique. At sixteen, Dominique realized that the innocent little girl was gone. Her reflection in the mirror showed tears streaking down her cheeks. She barely recognized herself anymore.

Hildale, Utah

Casey screamed at the top of her lungs as another thunderbolt of pain shot through her abdomen and radiated to her back. "I think something is wrong," the midwife said with a look of terror on her face.

"What could it be?" Casey's husband, Samson, asked, his eyes as wide as marbles.

"I think the baby is upside down . . . breach," the midwife answered, wiping sweat from her brow.

"Help me!" Casey screamed out again, her face turning the color of a beet. Her body dripped with sweat.

"What do we do?" Samson asked, nervously pacing the room. If this baby didn't make it, this would be the third child Casey had lost since they'd been married three years ago. Samson thought it was a curse from God. After the second baby, he had started to regret marrying Casey. When she'd locked herself in the bathroom of the temple for three hours on the day of their wedding, he should have taken that as an ill omen. The prophet had ordered the door taken down and Casey had to be physically taken to the altar for the ceremony.

"We will have to take her to the hospital or the baby will die. She needs a caesarean section," the midwife said gravely, her wrinkled hands shaking fiercely.

Casey screamed again, arching her body on the bed, the pain stabbing through her back and around her middle. The midwife rushed to Casey's side and dabbed her head with a wet towel. Everything in the room had been prepared for the delivery. Hot water sat on a small homemade wooden table, towels lay in wait on the end of the bed and a small handmade straw basket sat prepared for its new occupant. None of the supplies had been touched. It had been ten hours and no change. The midwife had tried to palpate the abdomen and turn the baby around, but she'd failed. The only thing she had accomplished was causing huge bruises to form on Casey's swollen stomach.

"You have to make a decision. I don't think she has much time," the midwife announced. Her long grey braid was soaked with sweat. She had delivered almost all of the babies on the compound in the last twenty years, Casey included. She knew from experience that the situation was grave.

"I will have to consult the prophet," Samson said, continuing to pace.

"Well, hurry then. There isn't anything else we can do here," the midwife replied as she tried in vain to comfort Casey. Samson ran out of the room. A few minutes later he returned with the prophet, Casey's father, and two elders. They all began praying in unison. The air in the room was thick and stifling. It was almost as if death was surrounding it, not willing to leave without its prize.

"Argggh." From deep down in her throat, Casey emitted a scream that was nothing less than primordial. All of the prayers ceased when the sheet covering Casey to the waist became drenched in dark red blood. The midwife pulled back the sheet and her eyes grew wide. A pair of tiny blue feet dangled from Casey's vaginal opening. Casey screamed again, feeling the uncontrollable urge to push. Her body bucked violently as the torso of the baby appeared, its head stuck in the lion jaw trap that was its mother. The midwife was shaking all over. She could hardly bear to look at the small, blue, lifeless form that emerged from her body. Casey bent to the side of the bed and vomited. Casey emitted a loud growl as she continued to push, letting nature take its course. The midwife closed her eyes and tugged roughly on the baby, twisting and turning the small body.

"Please, make it stop!" Casey screamed, rattling the walls of the small room. Finally, the baby was free. There were no cries. Time seemed to stand still. Casey collapsed on the bed like a lifeless rag doll. Samson ran to her side, refusing to look at his dead son. After having eight girls by his other wives, he was heartbroken to have lost his son. The rest of the men filed out of the room, flanking the prophet who had instructed Samson not to take his wife to the hospital.

"I want to see it," Casey whispered, barely able to speak, so weak from the amount of blood she'd lost. The midwife nodded, sorrow written into her face just as naturally as the wrinkles. She gently swaddled the baby in blankets that Casey's sister wives had knitted by hand. The baby had been cleaned up, his small arms folded across his tiny chest.

The midwife moved slowly, holding the small bundle. When she was at Casey's bedside, she placed the baby up against Casey's chest, where he would've gone to suckle if he were alive. Casey took a weak hand and touched the little angelic face. "Christopher," she whispered. The midwife looked at her confused. "That is his name . . . Christopher," Casey said, tears cascading down her face, landing in rivulets on her son's lifeless form. The midwife nodded her understanding. Casey held the baby for three more hours. Weak and fading, she rocked him until her body and mind finally gave out and sleep overcame her. Casey slept for two days after that.

Harlem, New York

Jordan sat in his room, counting his money. He smiled when he got to $10,000. "Almost enough," he mumbled. He had been stashing to get his own place. He'd already gotten a new whip and his mother hadn't been on his ass so much lately. C-Lo had been right: scared niggahs don't make money, real niggahs take money. Jordan had been under C-Lo's tutelage for three years and he had made more money than he'd ever seen in his entire life.

C-Lo had decided it would be a waste to put Jordan on to slanging rocks; instead, he had told Jordan that his education and schoolboy charm would come in handy in a different way. It was Jordan's job to recruit "young bitches" for C-Lo's stable. With his Morris Chestnut likeness, it wasn't that hard a job for Jordan. All the years his mother had called him a black bastard, black cockroach, ugly black gorilla, dark curse, etc. had made Jordan think his complexion, which resembled smooth, dark coal, was ugly and unattractive to the females. But the girls he was able to catch oftentimes told him he was "fine" and "sexy as hell." C-Lo paid Jordan a handsome fee for each girl he brought into the stable. Jordan thought it was the easiest job on earth. He'd seen C-Lo make other dudes on his payroll work much harder for way less cake. Jordan just took it to mean that C-Lo liked him more than the other chump-ass dudes.

Jordan's cell phone rang, interrupting his money counting. "Hello," Jordan answered, placing his money back in his safe.

"I got a job for you," C-Lo said, without greeting Jordan with hello or any pleasantries. "Meet me at the uptown spot," C-Lo instructed.

"A'ight," Jordan agreed, grabbing his new car keys off the dresser. He smiled, immediately excited.

Any other time C-Lo had said he had a job for him, Jordan found himself doing something easy like stepping to a little girl C-Lo had identified as one who "needed a daddy." Jordan would stake the little girl out, and follow her for a couple of days to find out information about her. Like, if her mother was a crackhead and she wore dirty or raggedy clothes, Jordan would step to her and tell her that if she let him get her a daddy, he would feed her and give her the finer things in life. Of course, he would use C-Lo's money to take the little girl out, feed her someplace nice and buy her a few new outfits. Then Jordan would bring her to C-Lo and shortly after that she would be on one of C-Lo's tracks.

Jordan pulled his Tahoe up to the building on 116th and St. Nicholas where C-Lo kept his uptown stable. On his way in, he bumped into Shanice and Dana, two girls Jordan had recruited. "Wassup, ladies?" Jordan asked. Both of the girls seemed to freeze when he spoke. It struck Jordan as strange that they seemed eager to hit the street. Most of the girls preferred to remain indoors. Jordan shrugged it off and continued into the building.

When he stepped off the elevator on the third floor, he heard loud music coming from C-Lo's apartment. "Damn, they partying up in this piece or what?" Jordan banged on the door. No one answered. Jordan banged again, harder this time. "Ay yo!" Jordan called out, cupping his hand around his mouth.

Suddenly the door to the apartment creaked open. The music got even louder as he stepped inside; it was like being in a club. There were two girls standing up against the long hallway wall, crying and shaking. Jordan furrowed his eyebrows and kept ambling forward toward the back of the apartment. The closer he got, the louder the music seemed. His ears hurt in the middle from the heaving thumping bass. Jordan pulled back the '70s style beads that separated one of the rooms from a small kitchen. He stopped in his tracks when he crossed the threshold.

"Close ya mouth, young blood. It's time to put in real work now, prove you worthy of making all that cake you showing off 'round this hood," C-Lo said, twisting his customary toothpick between his teeth.

"Yeah, I'm down, wa . . . wassup?" Jordan stammered as he took in the scene, his heart racing like fifty horses at the Yonkers Raceway.

"You see this here. This a bitch ain't got no class and can't be taught none," C-Lo hissed, walking over and using his foot to nudge the heap of flesh that Jordan couldn't recognize through all of the bruises, blood, feces, and vomit she was lying in.

"What . . . um . . . what she do?" Jordan asked, looking away, his eyes wide.

He couldn't look at her. Between the smell of putrid body fluids and the feeling in his inner ear from the music's bass, Jordan was starting to feel lightheaded, and his body began to sway a bit.

"It ain't what she do, young blood. It's what she ain't do,"

C-Lo replied. "See, when I was a boy, my daddy told me a woman is like a dog . . . once a bitch gets useless to you and don't serve no purpose, she gots to go. Ain't no use in feeding a worthless bitch. A worthless bitch, dog or human, gotta be put down," C-Lo continued, taking his toothpick out of his mouth to laugh.

Jordan swallowed hard because he knew what C-Lo was telling him he had to do. A cold sweat broke out all over Jordan's body. He could deal with gaming girls into C-Lo's stable, but murder wasn't part of the plan. Jordan's stomach churned, and he felt like he was going to either throw up or shit his pants.

"You ain't bitchin' up on me, is you, young blood?" C-Lo asked, walking close to Jordan and squeezing his shoulder like an athletic coach getting his player ready for a big game.

"Um, nah, I'm good," Jordan lied, squeezing his ass cheeks together to keep from crapping in his pants.

"I didn't think so . . . not as much as you owe me," C-Lo said, bending down, grabbing the girl's hair and turning her face up toward Jordan.

Jordan sucked in his bottom lip and scrunched his face at the sight. There was dark blood covering her entire face and her eyes were swollen shut. She let out a low moan. C-Lo threw her head down, letting it hit the hardwood floor.

"Here ya go, young blood," C-Lo said, passing Jordan a 9 mm glock. "You do know how to put a bitch outta her misery, don't you?" C-Lo asked, shoving Jordan in his back. Jordan's chest heaved and his hands shook. His feet were rooted to the floor; he couldn't move even if he wanted to. "Let's go, young blood. This ain't that fuckin' hard!" C-Lo barked.

Stepping in front of Jordan, C-Lo bent down, lifted the girl's head up off the floor and grabbed Jordan's arm, pulling him down slightly. "Put that gat to her fuckin' dome and pull the goddamn trigger," C-Lo growled in Jordan's ear. The music, the smell, the girl's battered face, it was all too much. Jordan had stopped breathing, he was sure of it. Everything around him seemed distorted, he couldn't see straight. He felt like he was having an out-of-body experience and an unknown force was moving him. He raised his hand and pulled the trigger. The shot reverberated up his arm, and he dropped the weapon like he'd just been bitten by a poisonous snake.

The girl's head was obliterated. There was blood and grey and white fleshy matter covering Jordan's sneakers and the bottom of his jeans. His vision started to blur, darken, and then went completely black.

That night, when Jordan had pulled himself together, he practically crawled into his house. When he clicked on the light in his bedroom his mother was standing up against his closet. She held his stash in her hands.

"And just what the fuck is this?" she asked, holding the stack of money like it was a baseball.

"Gimme my shit!" Jordan lunged at her.

"Or else what, black spook? You gonna hit me?" Trina asked.

Jordan was stopped dead in his tracks. His stomach churned with fire. The last time he had gotten bold enough to get up in his mother's face, his two brothers had beaten him so severely he didn't think he would've survived the kind of pain he was in.

"Yo . . . I give you a cut of everything I fuckin' make!" Jordan screeched.

"Is this what you're reduced to? You out there pimping!" she barked, her face filling with blood.

"Fuck you! You are never satisfied," he growled.

"Do you know what I had to do to put you through school, you black monster? I had to sell my ass . . . I had to suck dick . . . yeah, I had to lay on my back and live on my knees!" Trina screamed, walking over to her son and getting right in his face.

"I don't give a fuck about you! That's where you belong . . . just like the rest of these hoes!" Jordan belted out, fighting back tears.

In a knee-jerk reaction, Trina slapped Jordan so hard his head whipped from left to right. Instinctively, he was drawn back to his childhood. He had vowed he would never be abused by her again. Jordan grabbed her by her neck and applied pressure as his face contorted with hate.

"You are the reason I can't even keep a job. I can't even take stand for anyone to tell me what to do. You made me the black monster I am, you ungrateful bitch," Jordan whispered harshly as he watched his mother's eyes start to roll.

Just before she passed out he released her. Trina crumpled to the floor, and her son grabbed what was important to him and stepped over her.

Chapter Five

Keeping Secrets

Dominique surveyed herself in the mirror one last time. The swelling wasn't as bad as she thought it would be, but the bruising was visible, even on her dark, coffee-brown skin. Using the foundation brush, she applied one more coat of makeup. She appeared to have aged over night. Dominique remembered a time when she didn't need makeup at all; her natural beauty was enough. She winced as she turned to check out the rest of her body in the mirror. She'd wrapped her own ribs with an Ace bandage. She couldn't go to the hospital because they'd have too many questions. She couldn't risk exposing her famous televangelist husband. *That's the price of fame*, she reasoned. Big stars probably never went to the hospital either; instead, they hired "personal physicians" to ensure their privacy.

Dominique and Alton's relationship had happened like a whirlwind. Dominique had been putting the pieces to her life back together when she met him in church—he had been a visitor at first, then became an apprentice. Dominique was at a very weak stage in her life and had vowed she would never let another man in her world. But Alton Camden was different. He seemed to be revered everywhere he went and it did not take long for him to build a following. When he had asked her out she accepted. It did not take long before he had asked her to marry him. Dominique had felt so unworthy at first. She had not been honest with him. She also had never experienced life the way Alton was providing, therefore, she put her past to the back of her mind and told herself she was worthy of being loved. They were married in a small-intimate ceremony. Dominique had watched Alton build his church from scratch, and now he was a television pastor almost as big as T.D. Jakes. The only difference was Pastor Alton Camden had a dark secret.

"You look beautiful, as usual," Alton said from behind her. Dominique jumped at the sound of his voice, spilling the brown liquid foundation into the white porcelain sink.

"Oh my goodness, Alton," she exclaimed, turning on the faucet to rinse away the mess before it stained.

"Don't worry about it, sweetheart. I will help you," Alton consoled as he approached her. Dominique exhaled. Alton was in a good mood. Right now, he was the man she'd married—a kind, gentle man. Dominique always counted her blessings that she was the preacher's wife. He could've chosen from one of the over 2,000 women who attended the church, but he'd picked her. She should feel grateful, she reminded herself. But in the back of her mind, she always wondered how he would react if he knew who she really was and where she'd come from.

Alton and Dominique rode to the church in silence. He insisted on driving, instead of using his driver. The smooth, quiet ride of his Audi that she normally found relaxing couldn't quell the uncomfortable feeling that seemed to come over her while in the car. Dominique kept thinking about Casey, and even Jordan. Since she'd seen Casey in the hospital, she'd come up with a million excuses to visit her friend again. There were so many things she needed to say to Casey.

"Casey, help me!" Dominique screamed as Jordan wound his

hands deeper into her hair. Casey simply stood there with a bland
smile on her face.

"She can't help you. You wanted to be a porn star, right?" Jordan
growled, forcefully pulling Dominique's skeletal frame.

"Jordan, please! I will pay you back!" Dominique pleaded.

"You will. Right now!" he huffed, his face in a deep scowl. Casey
stood by, a vacant look in her eyes.

"Suck it!" Jordan commanded.

"Jordan, no, please!" Dominique begged, her face a cakey mess
of blood, tears and makeup. Jordan cocked his gun and placed it
at Dominique's temple. She looked up at Casey, her eyes full of
questions. Why wasn't Casey helping her? What had she done to
deserve this?

"You ready to praise the Lord?" Alton asked, reaching for
Dominique's hand.

Startled out of her thoughts, Dominique smiled. "Yes, Alton.
I am ready," she said, turning her head to gaze out the window.
Tears stung her eyes. The one thing Dominique looked
forward to was that it was the third Sunday in the month,
so Alton would be out until late evening preaching and
recording at other churches. He never allowed her to attend
these speaking engagements. "Go home and prepare for my
arrival," he'd instruct her. And she always did as she was told.
This third Sunday, however, would be different.

"So, what's up?" Brice asked his little sister, looking at
her across the table of the crowded restaurant. Since Brice
had left home and landed the promotion, he didn't have as
much time to spend with Ciara as he used to. But he usually
made it a point to have some alone time with his baby sister
at least once a month. Brice looked forward to spending time
with his sister, even if it involved escorting her to downtown

Brooklyn stores for the latest sneakers or the newest gadgets that were hot with the teenagers. Brice didn't mind if Ciara broke his pockets as long as he knew she was safe and happy. Now that he was investigating the cold case murder of a young girl found dead in a Dumpster, he felt even more protective of his sister.

"Nothing is up. Why you always asking me that question as soon as we alone?" Ciara replied in typical teenager fashion, rolling her eyes and folding her arms across her chest.

"Ay, ay . . . what's that attitude all about?" Brice asked, looking at his baby sister in a new light. *Maybe she is angry with me because I haven't had time for her lately.*

"I know Mommy told you," she snapped, rolling her eyes. His mother had indeed told him. Ciara had not come home until two A.M.. the other night. When confronted about her whereabouts, she shoved her mother and ran to her room. This was not typical behavior for Ciara. Although Brice wanted to shake the truth out of his sister, he tried to remain calm in his questioning.

"Well, I'm waiting for you to tell me your version," Brice replied, keeping his voice even.

"You're my brother . . . not my father. I don't have to tell you nothing," Ciara spat, pushing her chair back and standing up. Her sudden movement surprised Brice.

"Where do you think you're going? Sit down," Brice instructed in a harsh whisper, trying not to attract the attention of numerous customers eating at Dallas BBQs downtown.

"I don't want to have these meetings anymore. I'm not one of your suspects to be questioned all the time," Ciara replied acidly as she headed for the exit. Brice dug twenty dollars out of his pants pocket and threw the money on the table before he headed for the main entrance. He ran out into the street and spotted Ciara's bright coat weaving through the crowd on the sidewalk.

"Ciara! Ciara! Wait!" he called as he picked up his pace. She seemed to ignore his calls and pick up her speed. Brice's chest heaved and his mind raced with questions. This rude behavior was uncharacteristic of his sister. She usually told him everything. Brice even knew when she had her period before their mother. Ciara usually confided in him about her crushes and even her little spats at school. If something was bothering her, Brice assumed she would have told him about it.

Brice caught up with her, grabbing her arm. "What are you doing?" he growled, holding on to her with an iron grip.

"Get off of me!" she screamed, wriggling to get free and managing to get some nasty glares from some of the patrons bustling up and down Fulton Street.

"Ciara, what is wrong with you? Why are you acting like this?" Brice gritted his teeth, wringing her arm to bring her closer to him.

"Ouch! Get off!" she screamed again. This time people started to stop and stare.

"Yo, man. The girl said get off her. You need to find one your own age," said a tall guy with a doorag and baggy jeans.

"This is my fuckin' sister. Mind your fuckin' business," Brice spat, still holding on to Ciara's arm.

"Who da fuck you talkin' to?" the skinny stranger asked threateningly. Suddenly, as if they grew out of the brick buildings, six other dudes surrounded Brice.

"I'm a fuckin' cop, so back the fuck up!" Brice warned, letting go of his sister for a second to pull out his shield. When he let go of her arm, Ciara broke free and began to run in earnest down the street. Distracted by the group of thugs, he couldn't run after her.

"Yo, man, we were just tryin'a help the girl. Ya'mean," the main guy explained with his hands raised in surrender, unwilling to challenge the shield.

Brice spun around to display his badge, hoping to disperse the crowd that had gathered to watch. Out of his peripheral vision, he could see his sister's pink jacket disappearing around the corner. He would be giving his sister a serious talking-to when he caught up with her.

Jordan glanced at the caller ID and picked up his ringing cell phone.

"Hello," he answered, a big smile pasted on his face. "What's the matter, baby girl?" Jordan asked, feigning concern for the ranting voice on the other end. "Hell, yeah, I can pick you up. I thought you'd never ask, ma," Jordan responded. He had already started to pull his jeans on. He always had time for helping a future investment.

Jordan got to Brooklyn in record time. He blew the horn of his BMW 750i and the girl came rushing out of the pizza shop on Jay Street.

"Hey," she said in a low whisper, ducking down in the soft leather seat of Jordan's car.

"What's up, baby girl?" Jordan asked, grabbing for her hand in a display of affection like he loved her.

"Nothing. I was just missing you, that's all," she replied,

"I knew you wanted me to be your daddy," Jordan said, trailing his index finger down her cheek.

"I couldn't stop thinking about you. I really like you because you are different and so mature," she said lovingly.

Damn. Jordan knew he had done his job. He had been stopped in his tracks when he saw her coming out of Boys and Girls High School. In fact, it was her unnaturally good looks that had caught his eye right away. Her smooth, caramel-colored skin; her long, almost jet-black, soft, shiny hair; and her slightly bowed legs and athletic walk had stopped Jordan short. When he saw her walking down the street, he busted a U-turn on busy-ass Fulton Street and drove back up to where she had crossed to catch the B46 bus on the corner of Malcolm X and Fulton. It hadn't taken much for Jordan to get her to speak to him and give up her cell phone digits. He hadn't intended to call right away with Casey's Fuck Fest filming looming at the time. But when Casey pulled her bullshit suicide attempt, Jordan decided that he might as well start planning ahead . . . just in case.

"Ma, listen. I'm glad you realize that I can change your life. I can go get any chick out here, but I hand selected you. A'ight, baby girl. So, now you got some big-girl decisions to make. Are you really ready to be with me? Just let me know soon, I don't like to waste time," Jordan spoke bluntly.

The girl hung her head. "I really like you. I want to be with you. You are so sweet," she said, wringing her fingers together.

"Well, shit. I guess that settles it then. I can be ya daddy," Jordan replied, smiling inside. "Let's go get some food and then go to my house and chill," Jordan said, reaching over and kissing her softly on the lips. He watched her close her eyes and relax at his touch. *She's all in. I ain't gonna have to worry about this one getting away.*

Casey opened her eyes and saw her mother's beautiful face. The pain in Casey's head made it hard to keep her eyes open. She felt a soft hand on her cheek. "Mother," Casey whispered, her voice barely audible. Casey saw snapshots of her childhood. The scattered good times . . . like when her mother had baked her a special pink cake and put a ballerina figurine on it for her tenth birthday. Her thin lips stretched into a smile.

"Hey, girl," Dominique whispered with a watery smile.

Casey opened her eyes. This time it was no hallucination. A hot feeling came over her body—fear mixed with shame. "Diamond?" Casey croaked, her throat feeling like she'd swallowed a handful of gravel.

"Yes, girl. What are you trying to do? Kill me along with you?" Dominique asked, smiling into her friend's eyes. She had forgiven Casey. On her quest to find herself, Dominique had realized just how much power they had both relinquished to Jordan.

"Diamond . . . I'm sorry. I'm sorry for everything," Casey rasped, tears sliding out of the corners of her eyes. She had hoped for the day that she could tell Dominique just how sorry she really was.

"Listen, you just try to get better. Don't worry about anything. I forgive you . . . the past is the past," Dominique replied with feeling. *The past is the past,* she repeated to herself silently.

Chapter Six

Escaping Reality

Brooklyn, New York

"I'm not going with you nowhere! I'm eighteen and I'm grown!" Dominique screamed as she stepped to Awilda. Dominique had decided after the last sex sale that she would no longer let Awilda make her sell her body. She was going to finally fight back.

"What you say, li'l bitch? Get the fuck dressed! Either that or your ass will be in the goddamn streets!" Awilda yelled back, pointing her finger in Dominique's face, trying to leverage the threat of homelessness against Dominique.

"Sell your own old stank-ass pussy! You think I don't know what you been doing all these years? Stealing my fuckin' social security checks, you bitch! I found the stubs from the checks. So where's my fuckin' money?" Dominique ranted, not backing down.

"Oh, you wanna jump bad? You think you could live off that measly check your bitch of a mother left behind?" Awilda asked, laughing at Dominique like she was a joke. "You didn't know that bitch fucked my man and got pregnant with you. Your grandmother took her side, of course, as always. You ain't know that ya daddy was supposed to be my husband, but your mother was such a tramp that she fucked him right in my bed! But she couldn't keep him either. You know why? Because she was a whore who didn't get paid!" Awilda spat, hitting her hand up against her chest for emphasis, spit and tears flying from her face.

Dominique's chest heaved up and down. She had never met her father. Her mother had told her that he'd died in a car accident right after she was born. She didn't want to believe what Awilda was saying. Her mother wouldn't have lied to her like that.

"I want my money!" Dominique screamed, pushing her bulky breasts into Awilda's chest. Awilda wasn't backing down from her niece. She let it rip.

"You think I chose to sell my ass? Huh? It was your grandmother who sold me to put that bitch of a mother of yours through school. 'Aleese is so smart,' everybody used to say. Then she got pregnant and disappointed my mother. And let's not forget when the good sister moved out and threw her nose up at us. But what you don't know is what killed the bitch! You ain't know that bitch mother of yours was a cokehead, did ya?"

Awilda's venomous words dropped around Dominique like small bombs, exploding in her ears. Dominique had heard enough. She pulled her fist back and punched Awilda dead in her mouth. Awilda didn't have time to react as her false teeth slid from her lips and hit the floor. Getting her bearings, she shook her head slightly and dug her fingernails into Dominique's face. Dominique squealed but held her own. She grabbed Awilda's hair and yanked her down toward the floor. They both fell. Awilda hit her head on the floor and Dominique's knees slammed into the hard project tiles. Dominique sat on Awilda's chest, pinning her arms down with her knees. She swung wildly, throwing a bevy of wild punches to Awilda's face and chest. Awilda's lip split as she struggled under Dominique's weight.

"You fuckin' dirty bitch!" Dominique screamed as she took out years of frustration on her aunt.

"Get the fuck off me!" Awailda thrashed, trying to break free. Suddenly, Awilda bucked her body upward, throwing Dominique forward. Awilda slipped from under Dominique and scrambled off the floor. She raced to the kitchen, where she grabbed a butcher's knife from a drawer. "You wanna fuck with me?" Awilda asked as she charged at Dominique with the knife. "You gon' die, bitch!" Awilda screeched at her, her eyes bugging out of their sockets.

Dominique ran toward the front door, fumbling with the locks. With the door flung wide open, Dominique raced toward the stairwell, taking the stairs two at a time down to the first floor. When she made it outside, she noticed her belongings scattered on the patch of grass outside the building. Awilda's shrill, hateful voice could be heard from the window as she tossed out more of Dominique's clothes and personal belongings.

Dominique ran across the street to the corner store and got a couple of plastic bags. Using her sleeve to wipe the snot and blood off her face, she hunched down and picked up as many of her clothes and belongings that she could fit in the bags. She walked down Fountain Avenue to the train station. Dominique held onto her pocketbook for dear life. Luckily for Dominique, Awilda had been so angry that she threw Dominique's pocketbook out the window. It contained all of the money Dominique had been stashing behind Awilda's back. Dominique had no idea where she was headed, but she decided to board the A train toward the city. Brooklyn held nothing but bad memories for her. Wherever the last stop was on the train was where Dominique would spend the night.

***

Harlem, New York

"Yo, bitch! You *habla inglés?*" Jordan asked, slapping Madi, the little Puerto Rican girl, upside her head like she was a little kid. The girl pouted and handed Jordan the stack of money she had spent the entire night working for. "Getcha ass back out on that track!" he barked.

"But, Daddy, it's daylight," the girl whined, addressing Jordan by the name he required her to call him.

"Madi . . . did you hear what the fuck I said? Ain't no fuckin' way you been fuckin' and suckin' all night and this all you got. A niggah was born at night, not last night," Jordan replied, flexing his jaw as he watched fear dance in the girl's eyes. She could barely stand upright. She was exhausted and her feet throbbed in the cheap high heels she wore. Just as Jordan was about to send Madi back to work, another half-dressed teenage girl walked slowly over to the corner of 116th and St. Nick, where Jordan and Madi stood.

"Daddy . . . this all I got," the girl said feebly, handing Jordan a small handful of crumpled bills.

"What the fuck is this? Hold up, hold the fuck up!" Jordan growled, rubbing his chin like he was thinking. "A niggah is being played for a fool out here," Jordan grumbled as he unfolded the bills and counted them. "You bring me a buck fifty and this bitch tried to come with two fuckin' bills after being out here all fuckin' night?" Jordan asked, incredulous. The girl whose name was Tasha but had been renamed "Tiger" moved closer to Madi. They huddled together, not knowing what to expect from their unpredictable pimp. "I got something for y'all . . . I see a niggah gotta make examples out here," Jordan mumbled under his breath, digging in his waistband.

"Wait, Daddy . . . I . . . I . . ." Tiger started, her eyes stretched wide. She never got to finish her sentence. Her body folded to the ground like an accordion.

"Ayi!" Madi cried, bending down to check on her friend. Tiger was out cold; the butt of Jordan's .40-caliber glock to the temple had taken her out. Blood leaked from the side of her head and Madi was afraid that Tiger was dead.

"Tiger!" Madi cried, shaking her friend's unconscious form. It was so early in the morning in this part of Harlem that nobody was around except the fiends.

"Now . . . let that be a lesson. Help that bitch pull it together and I'll be back for my dough in a few hours," Jordan said before he sped away in his car.

Jordan pulled around the corner, stopped his car and took a deep breath. It took a lot for him to be the way he was. Violence was never his strong suit, but he knew his reputation depended on it. He popped his glove compartment, removed a fresh bottle of Mylanta and took it to the head. "Ah!" he winced as the smooth liquid coated his stomach. His ulcers were killing him. Jordan had developed them after the incident with C-Lo and the girl. Once Jordan had taken care of a problem for C-Lo, he had let Jordan "fly," as he put it, and Jordan was able to get his own stable of chicks. Jordan had learned his pimp game from the best and he was already making a name for himself around Harlem. But Jordan made sure he was careful not to put his chicks on any of C-Lo's tracks. C-Lo had warned him against it and Jordan knew firsthand what C-Lo was capable of if he went against his wishes.

Jordan drove, lost in thought. He was on his way home, but wanted to stop at a breakfast spot and get some grub. Since he'd moved out of his mother's house, he often missed having a home-cooked meal, no matter how few and far between they were. "Look at that," Jordan said out loud, stopping his car short as he noticed a gorgeous, chocolate-colored young girl standing on the corner of West 113th Street looking lost as hell. She held a small folded piece of paper in her hands, which she was checking against the street signs. The girl picked up two plastic bags and began walking. Jordan sized up her. *Probably a twenty-eight waist; thirty-six C cup; and about thirty-nine around the hips.*

Jordan was a female body connoisseur, they were his commodity; therefore, he had to know his shit. Jordan turned down the street the girl was on. He followed her discretely, researching as he went. He took another swig of his Mylanta; he couldn't let the burning in his stomach mess his game up. Jordan rolled down the window on his newly upgraded Lexus Coupe.

"Hello," he called out of the window. The girl jumped slightly and turned to look at him. She wrinkled her eyebrows and kept walking. She looked like she'd had a rough night. Jordan noticed that her hair was a little wild and she walked like she was half limping. *Looks like a chick who needs a daddy.*

"It's like that?" Jordan asked, inching his car along the street as the girl walked and scanned the buildings for their numbers. "You got a name?" Jordan asked. The girl continued ignoring him. He could see her looking out of the corner of her eye. "Okay . . . I'll leave you alone then. But my name is Jordan Bleu . . . with the 'e' before the 'u,'" he shouted. The girl smirked. Jordan was apparently breaking through. "See . . . you know my name, why can't I know yours?" he continued.

The girl finally stopped walking. "Look, I don't talk to strangers, a'ight? Now you can keep it movin'," she said dismissively.

"Ahhh, keep it movin'," Jordan repeated. "You from Brooklyn, ain't you?" Jordan asked, flashing his pearly white teeth.

"How can you tell that?" the girl asked, surprised.

"See that? Now you wanna talk to me," Jordan teased.

"A'ight then . . . I won't," she replied, turning toward the address she was looking for.

"Damn, baby girl. Who done pissed in your Cheerios?" Jordan replied, using a line he'd heard before.

The girl glared his way, clearly not impressed. "You thought of that one all by yourself?" she asked sarcastically.

"Well at least I got you to give a little smile. Now if I can get a name, I'd say we made progress," Jordan said affably.

"Dominique. Happy now?" she asked, finally stopping and putting her bags down.

Jordan pulled his car over and got out. He walked over to Dominique. She was pretty in the face, with a small button nose and huge chestnut-brown doe eyes. *A darker Halle Berry.*

"So, *Dominique,* what is a little, gorgeous Brooklyn girl like you doin' uptown, standing outside the Wanderer's Inn?" Jordan asked.

"I'm visiting," she answered, lowering her eyes. Close up, Jordan noticed the scratches on her face and slight bruising under her eye.

"You running from the niggah who did that to ya face?" Jordan asked abruptly, not holding back. *Yup, she definitely needs a daddy.*

"For your information—" Dominique started defensively.

"Shhh, listen, baby girl . . . you ain't got to explain nothing to me," Jordan began, placing his finger up to his lips. Dominique stopped talking and rolled her eyes, feeling the heat of embarrassment rise up her neck. "I think you're beautiful. No, you are more like a rare, precious gem . . . like a diamond. If you want a tour guide during your visit," Jordan said, putting up two fingers on each hand and bending them quickly, making the quotation sign, "or if you just want to talk about things sometime, call me . . . Ms. Diamond," he continued, handing her a business card. *Jordan Bleu, Talent Scout.* Jordan was a business man and always prepared for moments like this. He bopped away from Dominique, letting her observe his swagger, and didn't look back until he had gotten in his car. Jordan started his car and turned his system up. His favorite Jay-Z song blaring.

You know I thug 'em, fuck 'em, love 'em, leave 'em
'cause I don't fuckin' need 'em
Take 'em out the hood, keep 'em lookin' good

As he pulled away, he could tell she was watching him, and he was confident he'd hear from her sooner rather than later.

Dominique checked in to the Wanderer's Inn for twenty-eight dollars per night. She figured she'd pay for one night at a time until she knew what her next move would be. Dominique had stashed away over $1,000 from all the times she'd gotten paid a little extra from some of her regulars. It wasn't a lot of money, but it was enough for her to get started looking for a "lame" job, as working girls called it. She had long since dropped out of school, so she knew the job hunt wouldn't be easy. She'd always been too tired to keep up with her school work after working long nights. If she got desperate for cash, Dominique knew she could contact some of her regulars and get it in with them for some fast money, but that might put her back in Awilda's earshot. Dominique had vowed never to see Awilda again. If that bitch's eyebrows were on fire Dominique wouldn't even spit on her to put them out.

The rooms at the tiny motel were dormitory style so she was forced to share her space with five other women. The women all seemed hard up on their luck. One older-looking lady sat on one of the bottom bunks, swatting at bugs that no one else could see; another tall, slim, young woman, with a cigarette hanging between her lips, stood rubbing her very pregnant belly and looking out the window like she was waiting for someone to come save her.

Dominique put on the meanest face she could muster and ambled over to the small bottom bunk bed in the far left corner of the room. Placing her worldly possessions on the end of the bed, Dominique sat down and fumbled with a fresh pack of Newport Lights. Unfortunately, she had taken up more than one of Awilda's bad habits. She hit the pack up against her hand to free one cigarette from the tight bunch. Placing it up to her lips, she heard the bug lady explode.

"There's no smoking . . . no smoking . . . no smoking," the lady hollered with a crazy gleam in her eye. Dominique raised her eyebrows and looked at her like she had lost her damn mind. The woman kept yelling until Dominique put her cigarettes away.

"What the hell? The bitch by the window is smoking and this crazy bitch ain't say nothing," Dominique cursed as she flopped back on the bed, too exhausted to fight about it. Forearm over her eyes, she told herself she'd just rest her eyes for a minute.

Dominique bolted upright as she felt someone touch her shoulder. The motel manager jumped too, startled by Dominique's reaction. "Hey! Calm down," the manager said. Dominique looked around, blinking. She must have fallen asleep. "It's time to either check out or pay another night," the manager demanded.

"What? I just got here late yesterday," Dominique said, rubbing the sleep from her eyes.

"Doesn't matter. New day, new pay," the manager responded sarcastically.

Sighing, Dominique went to grab her pocketbook, which she had laid on the bed. She had meant to secure it under her pillow but her exhausted body made it impossible to think clearly. Feeling around frantically, Dominique came up empty. A sharp pain stabbed her in the abdomen.

"Wait . . . where is my shit?" Dominique screamed, looking around the room frantically, the panic setting in. Her little plastic bags and pocketbook were gone! Everything she had to her name had been in those bags. "Somebody took all of my shit!" Dominique exclaimed, her legs wobbly as she rustled the covers off her rented bed, hoping her items would magically appear.

"That has nothing to do with me," the manager said, throwing her hands up dismissively.

"Where the fuck are the bitches who were in here? You let someone leave with my shit!" Dominique belted out, a huge lump forming in her throat and tears burning at the backs of her eyes. Everybody who had been in the room when Dominique arrived, with the exception of the bug lady, was gone. "Who took my shit?" Dominique screamed, rushing over to the bug lady. The lady's hazy blue dilated pupils were glassy and beady like a cat's. Dominique shook the little crazy lady's shoulders.

"She doesn't talk, so you are out of luck there," the manager told Dominique.

"Y'all gonna have to do something . . . you fuckin' let somebody leave with my shit!" Dominique cried, sweat dripping down her back.

"Look, you pay or leave . . . you decide," the manager replied without sympathy.

"Pay with what?" Dominique shrieked, digging into her back pocket. All that was there was Jordan's card and three single dollar bills—change from a five she'd broken to get a soda on her way here.

"I will give you an extra hour to get out . . . but no longer than that," the manager said, turning and dragging her swollen feet out of the room. Dominique slumped back down on the bed and put her head in her hands. What was she going to do now?

Dominique took the extra time the lady had given her to take a shower. Although she had to put back on the same dirty clothes she arrived in, at least her body wouldn't feel so grimy. Dominique stepped out of the motel, looking down the residential block. There was only one way that she instinctively knew how to make fast money. Dominique told herself she would do it this one time and then she'd set out to find a regular job, even if it was sweeping up at McDonald's.

She walked two blocks to a small bodega and asked for quarters in exchange for her three dollars. She used seventy-five cents to buy three bags of pretzels. She was starving. She stuffed her mouth with a few pretzels and walked until she found a pay phone, which were few and far between with the emergence of cell phones. Dominique lifted the receiver, wiped it on her pants, and dialed the only number she could remember. It was one of her regulars who usually came to pick her up at Awilda's house in Brooklyn. Dominique started thinking of a story to tell him to get him to come to Harlem so they could score and she could make some loot. She pumped her coins in the phone and dialed.

"Wassup, papi?" she cooed into the dirty public phone when the man answered.

"Ah, mami, my sweet thang," Gordo, the man on the other end, replied with his thick Dominican accent.

Dominique rolled her eyes, thinking of his fat, hairy-ass stomach and his little inchworm dick. "I wanna see you," she whined. He was a quick lay at least. Last time they were together, he barely lasted three minutes. That's what Dominique liked most about him; he got off on her real fast.

It didn't take much convincing for Gordo to agree to come uptown. He agreed to pick her up right in front of the Apollo Theater. She told him she would explain why she wasn't in Brooklyn when he got there.

Gordo pulled up in his colorful, pieced-together mini-van. Dominique had heard that Dominicans made their cars, but now she knew the shit was true for sure.

"Where ju wanna go?" Gordo asked, licking his lips.

"You wanna get a hotel room?" Dominique asked coyly.

"Mami, I know no nuthin' about Harlem," he said, rolling the "r" in Harlem.

"Well, I don't want to go to Brooklyn," Dominique said somberly.

"Wassup? Where ju auntie?" Gordo asked. He knew Awilda was never that far when he had his "dates" with Dominique. Awilda had secretly warned him that he better not try any freaky shit with her niece, so Awilda's whereabouts were of great interest to him right now.

"She's around," Dominique answered evasively. She reached over and began rubbing his flaccid penis through his pants, quickly changing the subject. Dominique felt his little piece of meat grow under her touch.

"How 'bout we pull over?" Gordo asked. He pulled his van under the FDR Drive, near the jogger's path. The elevated highway shaded them from onlookers.

"That's cool," Dominique agreed. At this point, she probably would've let him have her in a public store window as long as he was paying.

Gordo pulled his wide body out of the van and went around the side. He flipped down the back seats, making room for their tryst. Dominique got out of the front passenger seat and climbed into the back of the vehicle. Suddenly, a strange feeling of dread washed over her, sending a shiver up her spine. *This will be quick.* She rubbed her arms anxiously, willing away the sick feeling in the pit of her stomach. She had never conducted business without the sick comfort of knowing Awilda was somewhere nearby on high alert. Dominique was alone now.

"You want a full fuck, blow job or what?" she asked, speaking like she'd heard Awilda speak so many times. Dominique wanted to get down to the real business at hand.

"I wanna different thing today, mami. Here . . ." Gordo said, peeling off a few twenty-dollar bills and throwing them at her. Money was no object for Gordo, who owned his own vehicle body shop that doubled as an illegal chop shop.

Dominique grabbed the bills and stuffed them into her back pocket. She would count them later. "Whatchu want then?" she asked hesitantly, hoping this bastard didn't want to tie her up or no freaky shit like that.

"Lemme show you, mami. Relax," Gordo said, squeezing himself into the back of the van before anyone noticed them.

Dominique noticed the large plastic garbage bags that lay over his seats. *This niggah got the nerve to be protecting his seats from his own nasty-ass cum.*

She worked her jeans down over her hips in the tight space. Dominique didn't take her eyes off Gordo as he fondled his dick. "You got a condom?" she asked, spitting on her hand and placing it up against her vaginal opening—the poor girl's lubrication. Dominique knew she wasn't going to get aroused enough to get naturally wet for his nasty ass.

"Lay down, mami . . . no worry. I got a wife remember," Gordo reminded her, evading her question.

"What the fuck that mean? There are a bunch of nasty muthfuckas out here . . . trust me. Show me the condom," Dominique replied, not backing down on that point.

"We no need it, mami," Gordo said. Dominique squirmed in the tight space. Between slipping on the plastic bags and the nuts and bolts of the flipped seats stabbing her in the ass, she was ready to be done with it. Gordo moved closer to her, pushing her flat on her back. He was on his knees and placed one on each side of her; straddling her as he stroked his erect penis. Dominique swallowed hard, her legs trembling fiercely.

"Let me do it," she volunteered, trying to come up on elbows under his weight. She couldn't move; Gordo had her pinned. She was thinking if all he wanted to do was jerk off she would get him there much faster. He placed his hand up, halting her movements. Dominique lowered her shoulders. Suddenly, Gordo started breathing hard and Dominique closed her eyes. *He wants to cum on my breasts.*

"Mmm," he moaned loudly, like it was about to happen. She closed her eyes. The next thing Dominique felt was warm liquid spilling on her face, her neck, and in her hair. The strong smell burned her nostrils. She jumped back, but Gordo's full weight pressed on her stomach, immobilizing her. He continued to urinate all over her. Dominique didn't scream because she didn't want to risk getting urine in her mouth. She thrashed wildly, throwing futile punches and kicking her legs. She was powerless under his weight. After Gordo emptied his bladder, he was so turned on, he ejaculated all over her.

"You muthafucka!" Dominique shrieked as he let her up. Gordo let out a high-pitched laugh.

"No auntie . . . anything goes! Now get the fuck outta my car!" he spat, pushing Dominique out before she could fully put her pants back on. Once on the sidewalk, she bent over and threw up.

Although it was fall, it seemed like the sun was bearing down on Dominique, angry and unforgiving. Her underarms itched with perspiration. The urine that had soaked her hair was now dry, crusting and matting her hair to her head. Dominique's legs were lead heavy and ached as she ambled forward. She needed to sit down for just a minute, count the money Gordo had thrown at her and determine if she had enough to get a room . . . at least at the YMCA. Dominique stopped at the first empty stoop she saw and sat down. She unfolded the bills and realized Gordo had thrown only one twenty-dollar bill, the others were one-dollar bills.

"Urgh," Dominique growled, gripping the money so tight her arms shook and her nails left moon-shaped craters in her palms. She was tired, mentally and physically. She rested her head in her hands and heard a sweet hum moving toward her. "Hmmm, hmm, hm." Dominique swore it sounded like the theme song from *The Jeffersons* sitcom that she used to watch on TV Land when she lived with her mother. Suddenly the hum seemed like it was right in her ear. Dominique looked up to find an old lady standing in front of her. The lady had a cherubic face; the only things letting on to her age were the small pockets of sagging skin under her eyes. She wore a white, wide-brimmed, straw church hat with a small white net that resembled baby's breath covering her right eye. She was wide, with an ample bosom and a box waist and hips. Dominique immediately took solace in the old woman's soft eyes.

"Excuse me, baby," the woman spoke. She was trying to climb the steps, but needed to use the banister to climb.

"I'm sorry," Dominique croaked out. Moving out of the way, she decided it was time to make her way to the Y for a bed. But something kept her rooted in place. The old woman made it up to the front door and fished her keys from her purse. Dominique sat back down and told herself she would just rest for one more minute. After twenty minutes had passed, Dominique still had not come up with a real plan. She didn't know her way around Harlem like she did Brooklyn.

"Listen, baby, I don't pry in folks' business, but you look like you having a rough spot right now." Dominique heard the soothing melodic voice from behind her. She turned around and swallowed the lump forming in her throat, willing herself not to cry.

"Are you hungry?" the kind lady asked. Dominique shook her head slightly, quickly wiping away the tears before they had the chance to fall.

"I'm Ina Mae Grady . . . Mama Grady to all the kids," the old woman whispered as Dominique followed her like a duckling follows its mother away from danger.

Mama Grady's apartment smelled like mothballs and peppermint. Walking in was like going through a time warp to the '70s. Although Dominique hadn't been born yet, she'd seen several of the items Mama Grady had in her apartment, like the oversized wooden fork and spoon that hung on the wall outside of the kitchen, just as she'd seen on television sitcoms.

"Let me fix you some food," Mama Grady said as she padded through the kitchen, dragging her feet like they hurt really badly. She opened up the old-fashioned Frigidaire and clanked pots. The sound comforted Dominique for some reason. It was like having a nana all over again.

"So where's ya mama?" Mama Grady called out from the kitchen to Dominique, who was sitting in the living room. Dominique was amazed at how many pictures Mama Grady had on her walls. *These must be her kids and grandkids*, Dominique thought.

"She's dead," Dominique answered, clearing her throat. She'd decided a long time ago that thinking about what her life would be like if her mother was alive was a waste of time.

"Oh, baby, I'm sorry to hear that," Mama Grady replied, her Southern drawl making Dominique picture the words dragging the sides of her mouth down at the corners. "C'mon here now," Mama Grady summoned. Dominique went to the small flower-topped Formica table and pulled out one of the old metal-back chairs. Ashamed of her appearance, Dominique asked if she could use the bathroom. She wanted to at least wash her hands and face before she tried to eat. "Right down there, baby," Mama Grady said, pointing to the doorway leading to the hallway.

Dominique walked down a small hallway and stepped into the small bathroom. Once inside, she looked around at the pink wallpaper and the soft, shaggy floor mats. The color and the coziness of the space made Dominique want to lie down. She opened the small medicine cabinet that hung over the sink; it was a bad habit. There seemed to be thousands of bottles of medicine. Dominique twisted some of the bottles so she could read them: DIOVAN, COUMEDINE, CODEINE, etc. Dominique was familiar with codeine and its effects. Awilda had given her the pills a couple of times to relax her. Dominique hurriedly stashed the bottle of pills in her sock, washed her hands, and rushed back to the table.

"You eat smothered chicken?" Mama Grady asked. Dominique nodded. She'd never had smothered chicken but it smelled delicious. Dominique threw her legs under the table and began devouring the food.

"Hold on now, chile, we says grace in Mama Grady's house," she corrected. Dominique hadn't said grace since she was thirteen. She placed her fork down and bowed her head while Mama Grady prayed.

When she was done eating, Mama Grady gave Dominique a towel and face rag. "Take a shower and clean yourself up. I will run the machine on your clothes," Mama Grady instructed, like she helped destitute children on regular basis. Dominique immediately peeled off her soiled clothes and handed them to Mama Grady.

"You sure you ain't been on the streets?" Mama Grady asked. Dominique's cheeks flamed over with shame and she rushed to the bathroom. Stepping under the rusted, old-fashioned showerhead, Dominique inhaled. The water felt so good on her body. She scrubbed until her dark skin felt raw and clean.

Although trust was not something that came easy for Dominique, she felt like Mama Grady could be trusted. Dominique stepped out of the bathroom into the small hallway, still toweling off her hair. She could hear voices. As she made it to the doorway of the kitchen, she noticed a woman standing in the living room. The woman turned quickly, startled by Dominique's presence. Her face was familiar. Dominique had seen her in Mama Grady's pictures; although now small crow's-feet drew in the corners of her eyes, and laugh lines outlined her mouth.

"Oh, Mama, not again," the woman sighed, her eyes hooding over, glaring at Dominique.

"Sharon, this girl was sitting out there burning up and hungry as a hostage," Mama Grady explained to her daughter. Dominique went still, her face burning under Sharon's glares.

"Look, you always helping these kids. They rob you blind and never come back. Mama, you can't keep taking in strays off the street. One day one of them gon' hit you over the head and I'm gonna come home to find you dead. Now, you ought to be more mindful of that. You're living in a different time, Mama," Sharon scolded, wagging her finger at her elderly mother like she was the child.

"This baby ain't got no mama, Sharon," Mama Grady mumbled in a low whisper, as if apologizing to Dominique for her daughter's behavior.

"I . . . I . . . was just leaving," Dominique stumbled over her words. When she looked at Mama Grady, her soft, almond-shaped eyes sparkled with sympathy. Dominique picked up her freshly washed clothes and went back to the bathroom to put them on. She picked up her stolen stash of pills from behind the toilet and placed them back into the medicine cabinet, determined to prove Sharon wrong about her.

Dominique walked slowly over to Mama Grady, under Sharon's close watch. She bent down and hugged the old woman's wide shoulders. "Thank you for everything," Dominique managed to squeak out, her tongue seemingly pasted to the roof of her mouth.

"Hmph," Sharon snorted.

"It's okay, baby," Mama Grady comforted, patting Dominique on her back. That touch of affection was one Dominique hadn't felt in years. The tears came down in uncontrollable streams. Dominique turned quickly before Sharon or Mama Grady could see her crying and she rushed toward the door. As soon as she stepped out, she could hear Sharon bolting and chaining the locks on the door. Dominique placed her back up against the cold, uninviting steel of the door, and slid down to the ground. With twenty-six dollars in her pocket, she had to come up with a plan.

"So, young blood. I see you on the come up. How's the pimp game treatin' you?" C-Lo asked, running his tongue over his fronts.

"Shit is goin' a'ight. I mean, it's just like you taught me. Bitches always gon' try a niggah," Jordan answered, sitting across from C-Lo in Amy Ruth's as they broke bread.

"That's good, young blood . . . that's real good," C-Lo complimented, pushing his food away and taking his tooth-pick from the top of his ear where he'd stored it before they started eating. Jordan smiled; he liked it when he received compliments on his work.

"Young blood, we need to rap a taste," C-Lo said, his voice suddenly ominous.

"Yeah, man . . . wassup?" Jordan asked, shifting in his seat.

"Word on the streets is you puttin' your girls on my tracks," C-Lo said, getting to the point.

"Nah, man. I would never step on your toes like that. I ain't that dude who will bite the hand that fed me," Jordan said, immediately copping a plea.

"I gave you one track in Harlem and that was generous. I told you take your bitches up to Hunt's Point or to grimy-ass Brooklyn," C-Lo said seriously.

Before he could finish Jordan cut in. "Yo, C-Lo man. I'm gonna find out who is runnin' their trap and I'ma fuckin' go up top on a niggah. I ain't gon' step on ya toes, man," Jordan said, looking upset.

"A'ight, if you say so, young blood. I always give a young dude a choice . . . they can cross me or be straight up. I'ma take your word for it, but if I find out you lied to me, you gon' have hell to pay," C-Lo threatened, twirling the little wooden splinter between his fish lips.

"Yo, I'm telling you I ain't lying," Jordan said deceitfully, looking C-Lo right in the eye.

"Like I said, I'ma take ya word for it, young blood," C-Lo said, knowing better. He looked Jordan up and down. "Listen, I'm having a party this weekend. Come on through," C-Lo invited, standing up and tossing $200 on the table, leaving Jordan there.

Jordan had to think of his next move—fast. He had just told a bold-faced lie to the most dangerous man in Harlem. Before he could come up with a strategy, his cell phone vibrated in his pocket.

Dominique stayed at the YMCA on West 135th Street for one night—it was all she could afford. The day after, she walked to 125th Street and attempted to apply for jobs at some of the stores. Dominique did not even know her own social security number by heart, and almost every application had asked for it. It dawned on her then that Awilda must have all of her documents—birth certificate and social security card. Dominique also didn't have a phone number to put down for a call back. What would she wear to an interview? Dominique spent the last of her money on food from McDonald's.

It had been three days since she had been in Harlem and each day since she had gotten Jordan's card, she toyed with the idea of calling him. He had said he was a talent scout. Dominique wanted to try to make her own way. Given her history, she was very wary of men. Maybe he was some kind of show business bigwig. People had always told her how gorgeous she was. Walking out of McDonald's, Dominique decided to call him. She would make an appointment just like anyone else. If she had to audition, she would. Unfolding the crushed-up card, she went to a pay phone, ready to take her future into her own hands.

"Speak," Jordan answered.

"Hi . . . this is Dominique. The girl you called 'Diamond.' I was just calling because I think I probably could contribute to your talent business . . ." Dominique rambled, the words rolling off her tongue heavily and clumsily.

"Whoa, whoa. Who is this? Slow down," Jordan said, furrowing his brow as he listened to the rapid string of words spoken on the other end of the line. "Oh, Diamond," he replied, finally connecting the dots.

"You remember me?" she asked.

Of course he did. How could he forget her and that look of desperation on her face? "Look, I can come pick you up. We will talk about my talent scouting business later," Jordan offered in response to Dominique's questions about what kind of work he could find her. Jordan could hear the desperation in her voice.

***

When Jordan pulled up to 125th Street he could tell Dominique had been through some shit. Her eyes were vacant and rimmed under the bottom, like she hadn't slept in a couple of days. She had on the same clothes he'd seen her in three days prior and her hair was wild, like a newly tethered bird's nest. Dominique walked over to Jordan's car like a zombie, her steps unsure, hesitation and distrust weighing her down.

"Damn, Diamond, what happened, baby girl? Your visit to Harlem ain't treatin' you right?" Jordan asked sarcastically. Plopping into the seat, Dominique slumped her shoulders, bowed her head and just fell apart. The tears ran and ran and never stopped. Without even knowing or caring whether she could trust him, she told Jordan about her mother; her aunt; and her most recent john. Jordan was all ears. "Listen, don't worry about nothing, Diamond. I can definitely help you out," Jordan said flatly, driving her toward his apartment.

Dominique had no idea what she was getting herself into, but even if this stranger killed her in his car, it had to be better than living with Awilda or living in the streets.

Arriving at Jordan's apartment, Dominique wasn't even afraid. She just desperately wanted to take a hot shower and get some sleep. Dominique told herself that she would not sleep with Jordan, nor would she stay at a strange man's house. All she needed to do was find out what kind of talent connections he had and get herself a job.

"Make yourself at home," Jordan said, opening his arms and welcoming her to his home. Dominique looked around in awe. She would've never known from the old building that the inside of the apartment was going to be so nice. Jordan must've owned every gadget imaginable. He had a sixty-five-inch LCD television hanging over an old-fashioned fireplace. The entire living room was decorated in light blue and brown. The chocolate-colored leather sofa and accent pillows definitely looked like they had a woman's touch. *He gotta have a girl or something.*

"You want something to eat or drink?" Jordan asked.

"Why you being so nice to me?" Dominique asked curiously.

"You look like you need a daddy, ma. I'm the type of niggah who can make your life right," Jordan said, handing her a glass of lemonade.

"A daddy?" Dominique asked, gulping the drink.

"I'll explain it all later. For now you need to wash because you smell like a straight sewer rat," Jordan said, chuckling.

"Thanks," Dominique said, heading in to the bathroom.

That night they stayed up late, talking. Dominique was aware of Jordan's phone ringing every twenty minutes or so. He had yet to tell her what type of talent scout he was. Dominique fell asleep on Jordan's couch. He covered her with a comforter and went to bed. Jordan knew he could play the nice guy for a while. He thought of it as a worthwhile investment that would pay handsome dividends in the future.

The next morning when Dominique woke up, Jordan was gone. She sat up and looked around, making sure she was alone. Dominique could not believe he would leave her in his house alone. He didn't even know her—she could be some psychopath for all he knew. Dominique looked around and thought about lifting some of his shit and running back to Brooklyn. He would probably never find her, she rationalized. Before the thought could settle deep in her mind, she heard Jordan's keys jiggle in the lock. Dominique quickly lay back down and placed the comforter over her head.

Jordan rushed into the apartment and went straight into his bedroom. Dominique could hear rubber bands popping and rolling. She heard computerized beeping noises, then silence. She peeked out from under her blanket.

"So you up," Jordan said, standing over the back of the couch where she had slept.

"Shit! You scared me!" Dominique jumped.

"I got you some shit to put on. You can toss that three-pete outfit," Jordan cracked on her. Dominique took the shopping bag and looked inside. He had gotten her two pairs of jeans and two sweaters. It was more than anyone had given her in a long while.

"Thank you so much. I will pay you back as soon as I can," Dominique replied gratefully.

"Yeah, you can pay me back by going with me to a party tonight," Jordan told her, tossing another bag at her. Inside was a beautiful black satin dress. Dominique took it out and surveyed it. She noticed the price tag, too.

"How did you know my size?" she asked him wearily.

"I'm a ladies' man. I can probably tell you your exact measurements. Now, get dressed and let's go get some grub," Jordan told her, walking out of the room so she could have some privacy.

Dominique was impressed. No guy had ever bought her anything without her first giving something up. Jordan hadn't even attempted to sleep with her last night. She wasn't going to front; the thought left her feeling somewhat disappointed.

"Dayum, ma, you lookin' right in that dress," Jordan complimented, making Dominique blush. She spun around so he could check out her assets. Her C cups and round hips made it look like someone had poured her into the dress.

Dominique had slicked her hair back into a neat, classy, bun simple, yet sexy. She had never dressed up in classy clothes like this before. The closest she'd ever gotten to dressing up was when one of her johns asked her to wear a costume.

Jordan bowed his head and slipped his obligatory diamond-encrusted Jesus piece around his neck. Rubbing his hands together, he checked himself out in the mirror. The all-black linen outfit he'd chosen was elegant against his smooth midnight skin. He reminded Dominique of pure black silk. His face looked so inviting, she wanted to reach out and touch it.

"You look real nice too," Dominique repaid the compliment. Looking at Jordan made her heart flutter and she had a feeling all over her body that she had never experienced before. Her face felt warm and her stomach churned. She now knew what the phrase "hot and bothered" felt like. Dominique had never experienced love before. She wondered if she could love a stranger so instantly that it rocked her off her heels.

Jordan placed his hand in the small of her back. "You ready, Diamond?" he asked, lowering his voice, the scent of his cologne and mint Altoids dancing in Dominique's nostrils. When he touched her so gently, Dominique was finally able to place her feeling. It was fear; an overwhelming fear, like someone who'd realized they'd just cheated death.

Dominique prayed all the way to the door that the bouncer did not ask for identification. She had never told Jordan her age, and he had never asked. To her pleasant surprise, Jordan did not wait in the long line that was wrapped around the building. Instead, he walked up to the front, nodded at the bouncers and he and Dominique crossed the threshold into the club. A thick cloud of smoke cast a hazy grey film over the place. Dominique hadn't had a cigarette since her last pack had been stolen, but the smell of smoke and the anxious feeling in her stomach made her crave one.

She looked around and immediately felt out of place. The bass from the music ripped through her rib cage, making her feel like her organs were knocking. The women in the club were absolutely gorgeous in Dominique's eyes. She felt like a rented date. Jordan noticed the look on her face and reached down to grab her hand. His touch sent a stab of electricity up her arm. "You a'ight, Diamond?" he asked, concern in his voice.

"I'm fine," she yelled over the music, glad that Jordan couldn't really read her mind.

"Stay right here," he instructed, letting her hand go. He moved like a panther, sleek and stealthy, through the throngs of partygoers. Dominique swallowed hard as he approached the bar. Dominique kept her eyes trained on him for some time, but after he stopped to speak to at least sixty people, she'd lost interest.

After some time, Jordan returned to her side with a long bottle of Grey Goose in hand. Dominique remembered the bottle and the taste of the vodka very well, because Awilda had made her drink it a couple of times to loosen up. "C'mon, I want you to meet my peoples," Jordan said, gesturing with his head for her to follow him. Dominique did as she was asked. She noticed more than a few eyes on her. *Maybe Jordan wasn't bullshitting when he said I looked nice.* Dominique didn't know how to take a compliment from a man who wasn't about to sleep with her.

"Ay, everybody, it's young blood. He showed up and graced us with his presence," C-Lo called out as Jordan approached his table.

"What, niggah? You thought I was gonna miss your shit?" Jordan replied, smiling brightly and sticking his fist out for dap. Dominique felt the heat of the man's eyes on her.

"You ain't gon' introduce me to your beautiful lady friend?"

C-Lo asked Jordan, his gaze fixed on Dominique. Jordan's face changed; his smile turned into a sneer.

"Oh yeah, yeah. Diamond, this is C-Lo . . . C-Lo, this is Diamond," Jordan said.

Dominique smiled and extended her hand in response to C-Lo's outstretched hand.

"I love diamonds," C-Lo said, kissing the top of Dominique's hand, leaving it a little wet.

"Stay and celebrate with me, young blood," C-Lo instructed, patting the seat next to him.

Reluctantly, Jordan sat down and Dominique followed his lead. He opened the Grey Goose and poured them both a shot. "Here . . . drink this and relax. You look all uptight," Jordan said, handing Dominique the small glass. She already knew how to take the shot. She felt a small explosion of heat in her chest after taking the hit.

"Who's the beautiful lady?" C-Lo asked, leaning in to Jordan's ear. He wasn't going to let it go and Jordan guessed as much. Since being on his own, he never brought his chicks around C-Lo.

"Met her on the street. Trying to feel her out," Jordan replied, leaning away from Dominique's earshot.

"I might wanna get to know her," C-Lo said, trying to gauge Jordan's reaction.

Jordan clenched his jaw and tapped his foot. "She is green right now. Runaway . . . Aunt tricked her out, I think. I'ma handle her and get her seasoned up myself," Jordan responded, trying to say "hell no" the politically correct way.

"Young blood . . . don't you think you owe me?" C-Lo asked, cocking his head to the side.

"I thought we were squared up," Jordan said. Thinking about the murder he had committed for C-Lo and all of the young girls he'd turned over to him, he'd more than paid him back.

"Look over there . . . we ain't never gon' be squared up,"
C-Lo said, pointing. Jordan looked on the other side of the
VIP section of the club and spotted his chick, Tiger. She was
sitting at a table nursing a drink. Jordan's heart jerked in his
chest and he shifted on the seat. "You know her, right?" C-Lo
asked.

"Hell, yeah, that's a bitch I turned loose," Jordan lied,
grinding his back teeth.

"Yeah . . . you turned the bitch loose on my tracks and she
snitched," C-Lo said, throwing his toothpick on the table and
taking a fresh one from behind his ear. Jordan was quiet.

"Cat got ya tongue, young blood?" C-Lo asked calmly.

"Yo, man. I don't know what that lying-ass bitch told you,
but it's not even like that. Let's talk about it later," Jordan
replied, putting his drink down.

"Yeah. We can talk about it later, like you said. But don't
leave until I get to speak with your little Hershey's Kiss," C-Lo
said, laughing.

A fire flashed in Jordan's stomach. He could have used his
bottle of Mylanta right now. "Let's dance," Jordan shouted
to Dominique over the music. He wanted to get away from
C-Lo.

"I don't know how to dance," she complained.

"Ain't nothing to it but to do it," Jordan said, pulling her
out of her seat. She smiled and followed him toward the
dance floor. Before they could make it, two of C-Lo's dudes
interrupted their stride.

"Jordan, C-Lo needs to see you out back for a minute," one
of them grumbled in Jordan's ear.

"I already spoke to him and told him we would talk later,"
Jordan replied, annoyed.

"Nah, niggah, he wanna talk to you now and he said bring
your friend with you," the other husky guy interjected, touching Jordan's arm. Jordan jerked away.

"I can fuckin' walk," he growled.

"C'mon, Diamond. I need to talk to C-Lo for a minute," Jordan explained. Dominique was there for the ride, so it didn't make a difference to her either way. Jordan followed the two men through a maze of people toward a small back door at the side of the bar. Dominique followed him closely. Once outside, C-Lo was standing with Tiger and three other men. Jordan squinted his eyes into little dashes and stared Tiger down.

"Young blood, I'm hurt. I'm seriously hurt," C-Lo started.

"C'mon, man, I told you . . ." Jordan interrupted. One of C-Lo's henchmen walked over and punched Jordan in the stomach. Jordan doubled over, blood immediately bubbling up into the back of his throat. Dominique flinched, her knees knocking against each other.

"Now, like I was saying. Your bitch Tasha here says you made her stand on a hun'ed and sixteenth and St. Nick. You know that's my track," C-Lo said.

"Yo, man. This bitch a liar," Jordan wheezed, holding on to his stomach, trying to will the pain away. A different thug from C-Lo's camp came over and punched Jordan square in the face this time. Jordan screamed, feeling his cheekbone shatter into shards under his skin.

"You wanna be a pimp? I'ma show you what happens when one pimp step on the toes of another," C-Lo said, stepping aside to sic his crew on Jordan.

Dominique covered her mouth now in shock. *Pimp!* Dominique could not believe she'd fallen into this trap. Dominique stood there watching, quaking like a leaf in a wild storm. She was afraid that they were going to kill Jordan. Her mind told her to run, but her legs would not move.

Another closed-fist blow landed to Jordan's face and this time he fell to the ground, unable to brace himself. The four men threw punches at free will, letting the blows land wherever they wanted. They kicked Jordan in the ribs and stomped on his thigh. One kick even landed on his chin. Jordan curled into a fetal position, helplessly jerking with every violent blow.

Satisfied that Jordan had gotten the message, C-Lo put his hand up to halt the beating. "Now, young blood, I want you to pack up your shit and get the fuck outta Harlem. If it weren't for your mother, I wouldn't be so nice. Next time I won't be so forgiving," C-Lo spat.

Walking over to where Dominique stood, C-Lo smiled wickedly. "Diamond . . . when you ready for a real man, you come see me," he said, grabbing Dominique forcefully and kissing her on the mouth. Her eyes popped open and she felt a small amount of urine trickle from her bladder. When C-Lo and his thugs left, Dominique bent down to see if Jordan was still conscious. It was the least she could do. When he failed to respond, she became a bit hysterical.

"Help! Somebody help!" she screamed into the night air. Jordan needed her just as much as she needed him right now.

Chapter Seven

Searching for Redemption

"I got her legs . . . you hold her arms," Earl instructed as their classmate fought under his strength.

"C'mon, sissy-ass niggah. Get ya dick out and fuck this bitch!" Earl screamed. Brice stood stock still. The three other boys were screaming at him to hurry up. He fumbled with his zipper, his hands shaking. Brice gulped the golf ball–sized lump at the back of his throat and moved toward the girl. She was flailing futilely, no match for their strength.

"Fuck her, fuck her, fuck her," the others chanted. It was like something out of a movie. Brice could hear Earl's Eddie Murphy–sounding laugh. It made Brice's ears ring. Brice climbed up on the bed, the girl's legs already forcefully spread waiting for him. He prepared to enter her against her will.

"Brice?" the girl's strangled voice sent chills down his back. It was a voice he recognized very well.

Brice woke up from his sleep, breathing hard. He squinted at his cable box and realized it was 4:30 A.M. He rubbed his hands across his face and flopped back on the bed. Brice often thought about going to a doctor for some Ambien to help him sleep. If he was drugged up, maybe then he wouldn't have such vivid nightmares. Brice hadn't seen or heard from his sister since their incident downtown. Maybe his worry had caused him to become a recurrent figure in his dreams. His mother still reported that Ciara was coming in late from school every day. Brice needed to get his emotions in order before he tried to speak to her again. Closing his eyes, he willed himself back to sleep.

Who was he fooling? Brice knew he wasn't going back to sleep. Walking over to his desk, he grabbed his case file folder and read over the notes he'd taken. Brice had gone out to the old crime scene where the fourteen-year-old girl had been found. The bodega owner told him about two months after her body had finally been identified, the girl's mother and family came to lay a memorial of candles and stuffed animals behind the store. The name "Arianna Coleman" had been spray-painted on the wall behind the Dumpster. Brice had looked up the family and was scheduled to meet with Arianna's mother today. He planned to find out all he could about Arianna. Brice didn't know if his fervor to solve the cold case had as much to do with making a name for himself in the department as it did with redeeming himself for his past.

Brice had grown up in the Kingsborough projects in Brooklyn. As a child, he had watched helplessly as his alcoholic stepfather beat his mother. Each time he tried to help her, he'd end up beaten up so bad that he'd have to miss school the following day. Brice took to the streets and started acting out as a way to vent his frustration with his home life. He and Earl Baker had been friends since before they were born. Their mothers had met in the free prenatal clinic downtown and realized they only lived a block from each other in the same projects. Brice and Earl were born two months apart and had literally grown up together. On each of their first birthdays, the other was the first guest to arrive. Before they started school, they had play dates when their mothers had face-to-face appointments at the welfare office, and when they started kindergarten at the same school, they had held on to each other like Celie and Nettie from *The Color Purple* when the school tried to put them in separate classes. Brice and Earl were inseparable in everything they did. For as long as each could remember, they had done everything together, including commit the heinous act of rape.

When Earl first suggested that they rape one of their middle school classmates—a special-education student who had a huge crush on Earl—Brice had told him no. But Earl always had a way of getting in Brice's head, calling him a faggot and sissy if he didn't give in to Earl's every whim. Brice remembered that day so clearly: the girl's screams; her vacant eyes after the third boy climbed off of her; and the fact that she never returned to school.

When Brice went to high school, he poured himself into his academics and Earl became more immersed in street life. The day Brice received his diploma, Earl got sentenced to three years upstate for armed robbery. In the time that Earl was locked up, Brice became a police officer. He thought that if he fought enough crime, he could erase his past. Brice had never shared his profession with his best friend or with any of his friends from the old neighborhood.

When Brice arrived at the Albany projects to see Ariana Coleman's mother, he already knew what to expect. The Bloods gang had had a stronghold on Albany for a couple of years now. Brice also knew when the gang members saw him in his swinging trench coat and wing tip shoes they would be so busy thinking he was there to round up the ones with open warrants that they would scatter like roaches when the lights came on.

Brice entered one of the buildings on Park Place and thought the inside looked worse than anything he'd ever seen. The glass front doors had no glass left in them. There were red spray-painted words all over the lobby, and the elevator button was completely missing. Arianna's mother had told Brice she lived on the sixth floor. Brice touched his gun to make sure it was there. He took a deep breath and prepared for his hike through hell. The project stairwells were a piss-laden hell, full of hypodermic needles, used condoms and the occasional scurrying rat.

Brice used his knuckles to bang on apartment 6E. "Who?" a small voice croaked from the other side.

"Detective Simpson," Brice responded. He could hear bolts and locks clicking open.

When the woman pulled back the door, Brice was surprised at how young she was. "Um . . . Bridgett?" Brice asked.

"Yeah, it's me," the woman said, noticing his surprise. "I know you're wondering how I had a daughter who would be sixteen, right?"

"I'm sorry. Was I that obvious?" Brice replied, blushing.

"It's okay. I get that all the time. I had my daughter when I was sixteen, but that doesn't make me any less worthy to have my child here with me," Bridgett said, her voice cracking.

"I understand," Brice replied. They both sat on the busted-up sofa. Brice looked across the small living room, which doubled as a dining room, and noticed all of the pictures of Arianna . . . how she looked before her violent death. She was a cute little girl. Brice swallowed hard, images of his sister coming into his head. *Life is too short. I need to make amends with her.*

"So tell me about your daughter," Brice said encouragingly.

"You know, from the time my daughter went missing, you are the first cop to ask me that," Bridgett said with tears in her eyes. "My daughter did not run away. I'm as sure of that as I am of my name. She had no reason to run away," Bridgett explained, standing up to retrieve some papers off the battered coffee table. She handed them to Brice. Brice surveyed the sheets. They were Arianna's test papers from school, mostly marked with As or Bs.

"Arianna was a good student. We had a decent relationship . . . I mean, she got in trouble for things here and there, but nothing major. Then all of a sudden, like within a month, she changed. She started coming home late from school. And she got angry all the times I tried to ask her about it," Bridgett said, dabbing at her eyes. "I had to work to provide for her and my son . . . I couldn't be here all the time. The last time I saw her, we had a big argument," Bridgett said regretfully.

"What about?" Brice asked, sitting forward.

"Arianna hadn't come in the house until after ten o'clock one night. When I asked her where the hell she had been, she told me she was almost grown. I will admit I was so angry and concerned that I slapped her and then she stormed out of the house," Bridgett said through sobs.

"That was the last time you saw her?" Brice asked for clarification.

"Yes, I reported her as a runaway to the police and I searched the streets for her myself. Three months passed and I continued to check at the precinct every day for her. They always told me they had no new information. Then one day, I got a call from a detective saying they had found my baby. They hurt her so bad they had to identify her by her dental records," Bridgett explained, looking at Brice pitifully.

"She had already been buried in Potter's Field by then," Bridgett sobbed louder. Brice was sorry he had conjured up all of these bad memories. "I just want to know, who would do something like that? Throw her away like a piece of trash?" Bridgett's fist clenched so hard her knuckles turned white.

"I'm going to try to find out who did this, but I will need your help," Brice offered.

"Whatever it takes," she said, then retrieved a small box from a back room. "Here are some of Ari's belongings. Maybe you can find some clues in there. It was too painful to look through it," Bridgett said, sliding a cardboard box filled with trinkets, papers, school folders and a diary toward Brice.

"Thanks," Brice said, looking down into the box filled with the teenager's junk. Brice wouldn't count it out. It may contain just what he needed to solve the case. Although he didn't promise to find the killer; he'd given her something she'd never had before—hope.

Brice took the box back to the squad and began the arduous task of logging the items into evidence. As he pulled out some papers to place them in a plastic evidence bag, a business card that had been trapped between the pages fell to the floor. *Jordan Bleu, Talent Scout.* There was a cell phone number listed. Brice went to his computer and ran an National Crime Information Center check on the name. It returned "no hits." He ran a Google search and came up with thousands of hits on Jordan Bleu—porn manager; amateur porn director; and an alias, "Jordan King." Brice entered Jordan King into the National Crime Information Center terminal. "Jordan Bleu, my ass. I knew I'd find out who you really are." Brice printed out a previous arrest for disorderly conduct with an address in Harlem. This cold case was getting warmer and warmer.

"Ay, Simpson, I hear you working the cold case of that runaway," Detective D'Guilio said, placing his hand on Brice's shoulder while he glanced at the file.

"You mean the case that you just gave up on after you heard she was a runaway?" Brice responded.

"We get a thousand runaways a month. She was dead and there wasn't no bringing her back," D'Guilio replied nonchalantly.

"Yeah, well her mother's not dead and don't you think she deserves some justice for her kid?" Brice asked, removing D'Guilio's hand from his shoulder.

"You know what, Simpson? Fuck you, I did my job," D'Guilio spat, storming away.

"Yeah, I'm sure you did," Brice mumbled, slowly removing items from the box.

D'Guilio rushed to his desk and dialed a number and started whispering into the mouthpiece. After a brief pause, D'Guilio responded angrily, "I did close it . . . he fuckin' reopened it." Flexing his jaw, he stared at Brice's back. He'd have to keep a close eye on this guy.

"Adult film star Denver Peaks, whose real name is Casey Pete, was released from the hospital today after an attempted suicide. Pete, who shot to stardom as the busty Denver Peaks in the adult film world two years ago, is said to be recovered from an apparent overdose of Vicoden, which doctors say has the power to stop the heart if taken in large doses. Pete had a fall from grace after winning a prized AVN award and having her next film do miserably in sales. Industry insiders say that when it was revealed she grew up as a member of a polygamist sect on the Backwater Creek compound that was recently raided, viewers shied away from the blond bombshell and her movies. Pete returned to New York producer Mikey Cuntmore to stage a comeback, but couldn't stand the pressure and tried to end her life in a dressing room on the set. Pete's manager,

Jordan Bleu, was interviewed after the attempted suicide, and said that she would be back in business shortly. . . ."

Casey seethed as she turned her television off. "Back in business, my ass," she cursed. Her heels clicked loudly against the mahogany hardwood floor of her luxury high-rise apartment. Jordan was nowhere to be found. Casey knew that Jordan had been there with company. There were two glasses in the kitchen sink and one had lipstick stains. Casey bit into her lip, thinking of his betrayal and abandonment. She'd had to call a car service from the hospital because Jordan had not come to pick her up. Nothing surprised Casey anymore. If Jordan could throw Diamond to the dogs, Casey knew she didn't stand a chance.

On the glass-top dining room table, Casey noticed three Polaroids sticking out of an envelope. Curious, she picked them up. Casey pursed her lips and shook her head. "Poor girl, she has no idea who Jordan really is," Casey whispered sadly. She knew the pictures were test shots—a picture of the face; the breasts; and the ass of a new potential porn star—or porn slave, as she saw it. Tossing the pictures back into the envelope, she flopped down on the couch, feeling all alone. But she didn't want to die anymore. In fact, she wanted to make things right with Diamond and her family, and finally shake free from her demons from the past, and the present, so that she could begin to look toward the future.

Chapter Eight

Surviving

Hildale, Utah

Casey ran as fast as her feet could take her. Her lungs ignited with every breath and sweat drenched her body. She could hardly see in the dark. Her brother, Ethan, had told her that if she made it to the main road, she could hitch a ride into town. He would be waiting for her there with the bus fare.

Ethan had been banned from the compound after he'd spoken out against the prophet. Casey snuck away to visit her brother whenever she was sent to the supermarket by her sister wives. She often complained to her brother about her mistreatment at the compound. After she had lost her son, Casey had suffered too much damage to her uterus to conceive again. Because of her inability to conceive, her husband viewed her as a curse and refused to be intimate with her. Since Casey was not allowed to have assigned time with her husband, she was charged with cooking, cleaning, running errands and taking care of the biological children of her sister wives. It was no secret that her husband had gone to the prophet and asked that she be reassigned to another man. The prophet had refused. It was her punishment for failing to provide her husband with offspring. Casey had had enough.

Ethan had convinced her to leave the compound for good. At twenty years old, Casey still had dreams of going to New York City to pursue her future at Juilliard.

By the time she reached the main road, she was completely out of breath. There were no lights on the road. After about ten minutes, she noticed headlights coming in her direction. Casey looked around nervously and placed her thumb out like Ethan had told her to do. The first car zoomed right past her. It was about fifteen minutes before a truck came by and it stopped. Eagerly, Casey climbed into the huge cab of the eighteen-wheeler.

"Where ya headed?" the burly driver asked.

"Town . . . bus station," Casey said nervously, too naive to be afraid for her life, but brainwashed enough to believe that people outside of Backwater Creek were evil. Casey prayed during the entire ride. The driver tried to make small talk, but Casey didn't know enough about the world to keep up. When she'd finally arrived in the city, she thanked the truck driver and scurried away.

Casey spotted her brother near the bus station and squealed in delight. Tears streamed down her cheeks as she ran into his enveloping embrace. It was a very real possibility that she would never see Ethan or Utah again.

New York, New York

Dominique rushed down Thirty-fourth Street, dodging bodies like a gazelle on the crowded sidewalk. She pushed her hands deep down into her coat pockets to hide the trembling. Zigzagging across Eighth Avenue, she spotted her ride. Dominique darted across the street and jumped in.

"Damn, that took a long time," Jordan complained, twisting his toothpick between his teeth.

"Niggah, please. Don't give me no lip. I'm the one risking my fucking life out here," Dominique shot back. She had just robbed a john of all his cash, credit cards and his Rolex.

Jordan smiled. "That's why I love your ass. You don't take no shit and you be making mad dough," he complimented.

"Yeah, yeah, yeah. Tell that shit to the next bitch who be making you money," Dominique said, rolling her eyes and turning her face to the window. Frankly, she was tired of the "life." She felt like she had more than repaid Jordan for his generosity. After they packed up and left Harlem, they decided together that she'd pull a few tricks—make some loot and open what Jordan called a "high class" escort service.

Two years later, Dominique was still pulling tricks but had moved up in the ranks. By now, she was also the head bitch in charge of some of Jordan's other girls. She didn't mind delegating work for others, but she insisted that Jordan abide by her one rule—no little girls! Dominique argued that there were enough grown-ass women willing to sell their asses that there was no reason to fuck up little girls' lives. Besides, they were too young at thirteen and fourteen to make their own choices.

When they were far enough away, Jordan pulled over so he could count up Dominique's take for the night. She handed over all of the money. Dominique felt a sense of allegiance to Jordan. He had basically saved her life. When she met him, she had been a used-up little girl, who knew about being on her back for cash by force, but nothing about running her own game or making her own money. Dominique didn't have a business mind back then, but being around Jordan made her start thinking about sex like a business instead of a personal act of gratification.

The first night she stayed with him, Jordan never even touched her. He just didn't know how much that had meant to her. Although Jordan had seen her as a potential money-maker, Dominique knew that his feelings had run deeper. In her eyes, Jordan had truly become her "daddy." In fact, he'd got in her head so deep that she didn't mind walking the track or robbing niggahs to make him money.

"Damn, Diamond! Youz a bad bitch for real!" Jordan whooped.

"How much is there?" Dominique asked, not really caring.

"A cold G in one night," Jordan said excitedly. He peeled off a few bills and stuck them in her bulging cleavage.

"For real, you need to get you some new bitches. I'm tired of being the breadwinner," Dominique said.

"Recruit some, then. You know you my bottom bitch...you can be the madam," Jordan said, laughing.

"I'm dead-ass serious, Jordan. I been selling pussy since '98 . . . a bitch is tired," Dominique complained in earnest. She dug into her oversized bag and pulled out a small, shiny business card holder. She removed a nicely wrapped weed cigarette and lit it. She needed to calm her nerves.

"What I tell you about that shit in my car?" Jordan asked, his mood changing. Although he wasn't into the drug scene, he never made her stop and sometimes even copped the weed for her. Dominique had picked up the pot smoking habit on her own. Jordan didn't object because it kept her calm and working.

As they crawled down Eighth Avenue traffic, Dominique put her head back on the seat. When they approached Eighth and West Fortieth Street, Jordan slapped her arm, ruining her melancholic mood. "Yo, look at this!" he shouted.

"What . . . what?" she grumbled, sitting up. Jordan was pointing to a little white girl standing outside of the Port Authority bus station. The little girl looked like an extra from *Little House on the Prairie*. She was dressed funny and kept looking around with a paper in her hand like she was lost.

"Yo, Diamond, word life, when I first saw you, you looked exactly like that!" Jordan said.

"Niggah, I wasn't wearing no damn flowered grandma dress," Dominique snapped.

"No, I mean lost as hell, like you was looking for a daddy," Jordan clarified.

"You better keep on driving and leave that little white girl alone . . . niggah, you really tryin'a go to jail messing with them," Dominique said.

"I'm telling you, she needs us. Can you imagine if we had a white chick in the stable? We could finally fox with those Wall Street cats and rich dudes who like the blond hair and blue eyes," Jordan said, his voice getting dreamy over the prospect.

Dominique was not impressed. They watched the girl for a few more minutes as people bumped and jostled her. "I'm not fucking with that, Jordan, so just keep driving. You want blond hair and blue eyes? Get one of those lazy-ass Puerto Rican chicks and buy them a wig and some colored contacts," Dominique instructed.

The next day, Dominique and Jordan left their Brooklyn apartment and headed to the city for another caper. Dominique felt brave enough to come back to Brooklyn with the protection of Jordan. But she still had not dared to return to see her aunt.

They had already stopped in Dominique's old stomping grounds—East New York—to collect the previous night's cash from the few girls Jordan had working Brooklyn. Neither of them were impressed with the take. Jordan threatened a few of them and then downed his usual bottle of Mylanta to calm his ulcer.

When they arrived in the city, Dominique hopped out

of the car in Times Square. She worked the side streets—the
clients paid more and were less likely to act up. Although the
city was under a change and Times Square was turning into
a tourist attraction, sex was still a high-demand commodity.
Dominique walked her block near Forty-third and Seventh
Avenue until she spotted a potential john. As she approached
the car, she noticed in her peripheral vision the same white
girl she and Jordan had seen yesterday. The girl was digging in
the overflowing orange metal garbage can on the street corner.
"Oh, hell no!" Dominique whispered to herself. "That's the
same white girl. Damn, she really ain't from around here,"
Dominique kept talking to herself as she walked toward the
girl. Dominique had a soft spot for homeless people, especially
homeless females since she'd been one herself.

Dominique approached the girl cautiously. "Hey," Dominique called out, a safe distance from the garbage can. The
girl jumped so hard, she stumbled backward. Her blue eyes
open wide, she slowly regained her footing and began walking
backward, her hands lifted in surrender.

"Whoa, whoa . . . I'm not trying to hurt you. You just
look like you need some food . . ." Dominique said, already
regretting her interference. The girl seemed to perk up at the
mention of food. "Where you from?" Dominique asked, taking in
the girl's outdated hairstyle and that awful homemade flowered
dress. The girl just stared back in silence. "All right, it's your
choice. I gotta go to work. I don't got no time to mess with
you," Dominique said, preparing to walk away.

"From Utah," the girl blurted out as Dominique turned her
back.

"Utah! How in the hell you get all the way to New York?
Shit!" Dominique exclaimed, whipping back around and crink-
ling her face. "What's your name?" Dominique asked.

"Casey," the girl whispered.

"Well, Casey, your ass is gonna get eaten up fuckin' with these mean streets," Dominique said, digging in her purse for a cigarette. The girl looked at Dominique strangely.

"What? People in Utah don't smoke?" Dominique asked, lighting her cigarette.

"I . . . I . . . never talked to someone with skin like yours before," Casey stammered.

"What the fuck you mean? They don't got no black people in Utah?" Dominique exclaimed, looking at Casey in shock.

"If so, I never seen or talked to any," Casey said so softly that Dominique had to strain to hear her words.

"Shit . . . no wonder you dressed like that," Dominique said. Casey looked down at herself, then looked at Dominique's clothes—a black bustier top that choked her breasts almost up to her chin; a jean skirt so short it barely covered her ample ass cheeks; and heels so high Casey couldn't imagine how Dominique balanced her weight on them.

"Well, I'm black and my black ass is about to feed you. C'mon, because I gotta get back to work," Dominique said, crushing her cigarette under her foot.

Casey followed Dominique closely until they stopped at a pizza shop right on Seventh Avenue. "Let me get three plain slices, extra crispy," Dominique ordered the food without asking Casey what she wanted. Casey probably didn't know anything about pizza anyway.

"C'mon and sit down," Dominique instructed. Casey obeyed. "So, farm girl, what in the hell you doin' so far away from home?" Dominique asked.

"I'm trying to get here," Casey said, unfurling her crumpled magazine clippings about Juilliard's ballet school.

Dominique laughed. "That damn school hard as hell to get into . . . plus, you look a little thick to be a ballerina," Dominique said.

"Thick?" Casey asked.

"Thick . . . yeah, like not fat but not skinny, either," Dominique explained. Casey lowered her eyes. "So you just came to New York . . . with no place to stay . . . nobody you know . . . and no money?" Dominique inquired.

"My brother Ethan gave me money but it was all gone before I got here. I had to stop in five different states and bus stations and everyone kept asking for money," Casey explained.

"What? You gave your money to beggars? Oh, girl . . . you are all messed up," Dominique told her, really feeling sorry for the girl. Dominique slid two slices of pizza toward Casey. She devoured the food.

"What is this called again?" she asked, licking the sauce from her lips.

"Ohh, lawd . . . where the fuck you been living? Under a damn rock?" Dominique asked, shaking her head.

"No, on a compound," Casey responded with a heavy sigh.

Dominique quizzed Casey on her life. She was truly shocked by some of the stuff the girl told her. Men having six and seven wives; girls getting married at fourteen; all types of crazy shit. Things that made her life seem almost dull. Dominique's cell phone rang, interrupting her interrogation. Dominique looked down at the screen and saw Jordan's name. "Shit!" she muttered, looking around. Jordan was going to spazz out when he discovered that she had not made any money. Then again, if she brought him Casey, maybe he would forgive her for not turning any tricks tonight.

Dominique and Casey left the pizza shop. Casey looked like she would have followed Dominique off the side of a cliff right now. "Look, I'm going to introduce you to my friend. Maybe he will let you stay with us for tonight," Dominique informed her.

"I . . . I . . . don't know. Ethan told me to go straight to Juilliard and not to talk to any strangers," Casey hesitated.

"Well, Juilliard is closed right now and you can't stay out here another night. You were lucky last night but it won't be like that every night. New York is a good place, but it can also be very dangerous for somebody as naive as you," Dominique warned. She was concerned about Casey, but also about making Jordan happy since her pockets were dry.

When Jordan pulled up, Dominique waved and smiled, phony as hell. She dragged Casey by the arm. Jordan's face immediately lit up. *Whew.* Dominique wiped the perspiration from her forehead, relieved that he was in a good mood. "What's up, Daddy? This is Casey," Dominique introduced.

"Hel . . . hello," Casey said, like a deer staring down oncoming headlights, without a clue of whether to run or stay put.

"What up?" Jordan replied, looking at Dominique askance.

"She never seen black people and since your ass is like a tar baby, I'm sure she is a li'l shocked," Dominique whispered to Jordan.

"What we doin' with her? Taking her to the spot?" Jordan asked.

"We need to take her with us. She won't survive one night up in that raggedy-ass apartment with those hungry-ass bitches if that's where you was thinking of taking her," Dominique said.

Jordan looked confused. This coming from the one person who was dead set against messing with the white girl.

"So you gon' get her ready to work?" Jordan asked.

"Let's just say I'm going to take care of her," Dominique replied, glancing in the backseat at Casey, who stared out the window like a kid at the museum.

When they arrived at Dominique's building, Casey hesitated before following them into the elevator. "Don't tell me you
ain't never been on a elevator, either?" Dominique asked.

"No, in Utah where I'm from, all of the buildings are one
level," Casey answered truthfully.

Jordan began to laugh, startling Casey. "Yo, you got two
weeks to break her in . . . get it right."

Casey had no idea what the black man was talking about.
Dominique looked Casey up and down, formulating a look
for her. *That hairstyle and that horrible-ass dress gotta go!*

Dominique showed Casey around the apartment and gave
her a pair of jeans and a tank top to put on. Dominique slapped
her own forehead when Casey confessed that she had never
worn pants in her life. "Those some crazy muthfuckas you was
living with," Dominique said, shaking her head.

Within three days, Dominique had given Casey a complete
makeover and she looked beautiful. When Dominique first
combed the long braid out of Casey's hair, her golden locks
spilled over her shoulders like rays of sunshine. Dominique
teased Casey's hair and gave it some body. Instead of the
customary FLDS bangs, Dominique flipped the shorter
hair into a layered Farrah Fawcett look. Casey loved it! She
swung her head around and smiled at herself in the mirror.
Dominique showed Casey how to apply makeup, too. Being
with Dominique was so much fun, and Casey hated when
Dominique had to leave her to go to "work."

Three long weeks later, Casey was ready to start working for
her own money.

"Okay . . . You remember what I showed you?" Dominique
asked.

"Yes," Casey answered, trying to balance on the high heels.

"It's just a date today. These guys are pretty smart, so don't talk too much . . . let me handle that part," Dominique instructed. Casey agreed with everything Dominique said. She was just happy to have found such a good friend. Casey thought of Dominique as her guardian angel and felt confident that she would keep her safe from danger.

The first time Casey was left alone with a "date," she thought she would piss her pants. She hadn't had sex since she lived on the compound with Samson and no matter how many times Dominique tried to show her the ropes. Casey didn't think she knew what to do—not their way, anyhow.

"Come sit here," the man said, patting the bed. He had told Casey at dinner that he was a stockbroker. Casey had no idea what the hell a stockbroker did, but she had noticed the wedding band on his left finger.

"Oh, what . . . this? I'm not happy," he said, his cheeks becoming flush.

"How many do you have?" Casey asked.

"What? Wives?" the man asked, furrowing his eyebrows, confused.

"Yes," she whispered, sensing already that she had said too much when Dominique had told her not to speak too much.

"Geez . . . only one. That's enough. Unless, of course, you want to be my secret wife," he said seductively.

I do," Casey lied, thinking about how Dominique had told her to move her hips. She straddled him and he eased back on the bed. Casey closed her eyes as her body moved with short, fast bursts of energy. She imagined herself dancing gracefully at Juilliard.

Chapter Nine

Rude Awakening

Brice sat at his desk going over the discoveries he had made while searching through Arianna's belongings. He'd linked the Jordan Bleu character from the business card with the adult film star Casey Pete and a girl named Dominique Branch. Jordan had managed both girls' careers. Brice felt a flash of heat on his cheeks when he researched Casey Pete, who was also known in the "business" as Denver Peaks—the busty star of a couple of the most popular blue movies that Brice owned. He had recently heard that she tried to commit suicide. Brice marked her name as a potential person of interest. He was both excited and nervous at the prospect of interviewing such a famous porn star.

As Brice jotted notes at his desk, he looked up to find Detective D'Guilio watching him. *What the fuck this dude want?* Brice was about to voice his question when his cell phone vibrated in his pocket.

"Hello?" Brice answered. "Wait, calm down!" Brice instructed as he grabbed his trench coat and headed out of the squad room.

Brice paced the floor in circles, beads of sweat lined up on his hairline like ready soldiers. "Sit down for a minute," his mother said, fanning herself. He was making her nervous.

"Why didn't you call me on Friday? I'm a cop, for goodness sake. You know how it looks for me to report my sister missing after she's been gone three days?" he reprimanded. His mother began crying again. Brice shook his head. "Ma,

I didn't mean it. I'm just upset and nervous," he apologized, grabbing her by the shoulders.

When his mother had called, Brice had been buried in evidence and paperwork regarding his case. Arianna Coleman's death already had him on edge, and now this. Brice had three squad cars out scouring the streets of Brooklyn looking for his little sister. His commanding officer had asked him to stay behind with his mother. They said he was too emotionally wired to be actively involved in the search.

It was so not like Ciara to run away. Brice couldn't help but think of what Arianna's mother had said: that her daughter was a good student and wouldn't have run away. But she had also noticed changes in her daughter's behavior—coming home late from school, angry all the time—changes that were eerily similar to his sister's. The entire situation made Brice's stomach muscles clench. He wiped his hands down his face and held his head in his hands, trying to be patient. Brice was torn up inside. Things like this weren't supposed to happen to his family. He had worked hard to get his mother out of the projects and into a nice brownstone in Bed-Stuy. He joined the police to help victims and their families . . . not to become a victim's family.

Finally, there was a knock on the door, from familiar NYPD patrol officers. "What's up, Simp," one of the officers said. Brice stepped out onto the stoop. He didn't want to upset his mother if there was bad news.

"What did they find out?" Brice asked, cutting to the chase.

"Man, her trail ran cold. She hasn't been to school in a couple of days. Some girl at the school said a guy in a big fancy car came to pick her up on a few occasions, but she couldn't remember the type of car or any other pertinent details," the cop explained.

Brice was rocking on his feet. He didn't even realize it. He suddenly felt a rush of heat and became lightheaded. This was all his fault. He had become so consumed with his career and hiding his past indiscretions that he didn't even realize his sister was in trouble.

"So y'all gonna keep searching, right?" Brice asked, blinking his eyes rapidly to clear the black spots from his vision.

"Well, we will turn it over to midnights," the other cop said.

"I want the whole fuckin' city combed! I don't care if it's street by fuckin' street! This is my sister! She didn't run away!" Brice screamed, the veins in his neck throbbing.

"Whoa, man . . . I will pass on the message," the lead cop said, turning to leave.

Brice punched at the air. His head pounded. He needed more information. What had happened to make his sister change so suddenly? What was she trying to hide? Brice tried to compose himself before he went to speak with his mother. He knew she would have a million questions, and he needed to find those answers fast.

Brice stormed into the house, rushing past his mother. Before she even had a chance to fire a single question, he headed straight for Ciara's room. Banging open the door, he began pillaging through her personal effects. Brice opened dresser drawers and threw clothes left and right. Next, he went into the closet and pulled clothes off of hangers and dumped a neat stack of sneaker boxes, looking for hidden clues. He even got on his knees and looked under her bed. When his efforts turned up empty, he pulled the comforter and sheets from the mattress and even examined the mattress itself to see if anything had been stashed inside or underneath. Brice was trembling all over. His anxiety was making him lose it. But he had to continue his search.

Brice walked to Ciara's desk and emptied the drawers. Papers sprinkled over his feet like large snowflakes. Brice pulled the last drawer out and spotted Ciara's diary. Brice bent down and picked it up, noticing that it was locked.

"Fuck this," Brice grumbled, picking the lock with his pocket knife. With the sharp metal edge, he cut the small piece of leather that connected the lock with the book pages. He flipped through the pages of the diary and finally came to a page that piqued his interest. His heart sank when he read the lines:

He said he loved me. He said he is going to make me a star.

He felt like someone had kicked him in the heart. Brice dropped the book and raced out of the room and straight past his mother.

"Brice? Brice? What is it?" his mother called out behind him.

Heart pounding, Brice used the back of his arm to wipe sweat out of his eyes. He was a man possessed.

"Here she is, my new girl," Jordan said, sliding two pictures across the table.

"Wow, she's a looker." The white man whistled appreciatively as he surveyed the shots.

"I'm not putting her on the streets. She is going underground . . . that new wave in porn, man—that young girl shit. She been with me for a few days, but we about to hit the L.A. underground scene. Plane tickets already purchased," Jordan informed.

"Well, I got three this time, man, so what you paying?" the man asked in his thick, "fuggedaboutit" accent.

"You know I need to see them. These customers are getting picky and shit. They say they want the little ones until they get 'em," Jordan griped.

"Well, after that last fuckin' close call, I go straight foreign now. These bitches come from the Philippines, Bangladesh, and those poor-ass countries like that," the man explained.

"Oh yeah, my Russian connection got some good ones too. Can you believe these bitches think they will be coming here to get a rich husband?" the man continued, chuckling.

"Good. I don't want no more bullshit. Especially when you get paid to do shit and you don't come through," Jordan told him.

"Ay . . . I did what I was asked. You know, everybody wants to get their fifteen minutes of fame, I can't help that," the white man said, his eyes hooding over at Jordan's accusation. He pictured the detective's eager-beaver face.

"Well, he better back the fuck off. Don't he know fame comes with a price?" Jordan said pointedly.

"Well, let's go to the warehouse so you can take the pick of the litter," the man laughed, trying to break up a tense moment.

Jordan waited for the man to leave before he got into his own car. They would never leave their chosen meeting spots together, just in case someone happened to see them.

Alton sat in the dark church basement. The only light came from the illumination of his private computer screen. The images flashing on the screen made his nature rise. He grabbed his throbbing tool and yanked on it roughly. "Mmmm," he moaned, getting off on his favorite porn star, Denver Peaks. Her perky pink nipples drove him wild. His addiction to pornography was growing, as was his appetite for deviant sex. He growled as he reached climax, warm fluid spilling into his hand. The shame came instantly. Balling his hands into fists, he banged them on the desk, making his screen flicker. He wrestled with these urges daily, but they seemed to be overpowering him lately.

Needing more, Alton did a Google search to find more of

Denver's material. He'd already watched all of her recent movies. In his Internet search, he learned that there were some films of her when she was younger. Alton loved young girls. He tried to keep his yearning for them at bay by indulging in pornographic movies and magazines. But he didn't know how long satisfaction from the fantasy world would last. His sexual urges sometimes kept him up at night. Once, he had decided to dispose of all of his pornography. He'd driven fifty miles to a park and set all of his books and DVDs on fire. But as soon as the material caught fire, he panicked; instead, he chose to salvage his vices. That day, when he returned home, he had taken his anger out on his wife. His secret and the shame made him uncontrollably angry.

"Bingo!" Alton announced when he found what the Internet had classified as Denver Peak's porn debut. Alton clicked on the link to view a preview of the film. He picked up his Bible and flipped the pages, tears welling up in his eyes. He had to repent. He must be punished for his sins.

Dominique sat at the long dining room table alone with two perfect place settings. The shiny onyx plates stared back at her like evil eyes. As hungry as she was, Dominique wouldn't dare eat without Alton. The repercussions would be too deep. Dominique didn't have much of an appetite anyway after she had seen on *Hollywood Insider* that Casey had been released from the hospital and that she planned on giving a tell-all interview to *50 Minutes* about her life as a porn queen and attempt to explain her botched suicide. The reporter had said that Casey was prepared to talk about her childhood, her rise in the porn industry, and reveal some of the dark secrets of the business. The thought of Casey coming clean about *everything* made Dominique queasy. She definitely had to ask

Casey for one favor—not to expose her. It was the least Casey could do for her, given their past.

Dominique sat at the empty table for over two hours before nodding off to sleep. Her dreams were interrupted by the ringing doorbell. It was 7:30 in the evening and she hadn't been expecting anyone, although Alton was usually home by now. Since she and Alton had moved all the way out to Dix Hills, Long Island, no one came to visit. Alton's church was in Brooklyn and his assistant conducted all of their business from that location.

Dominique padded toward the entrance, trying to peek through the slim glass panels at either side of the front door. She could see that it was a man. "Can I help you?" she called out, not daring to open the door. She still had not figured out how Jordan had found her phone number when Casey had attempted suicide.

"Ms. Camden . . . um . . . Dominique Branch. I'm Detective Brice Simpson," Brice yelled from the other side of the door. Dominique's heart raced painfully and her knees buckled slightly. She immediately began to think the worst. Alton was in a car accident. Someone was dead.

"Yes," she confirmed.

"I need to speak with you. It's very important," Brice yelled from the other side of the door, placing his badge up to the glass so she could be sure of his identity.

Dominique pulled open the door. She was blinking a mile a minute and her upper lip quivered. She looked at the detective from head to toe. He was taller than Alton. Dominique had a bad habit lately: she judged every man she came into contact with on whether they possessed things different or the same as Alton.

"Sorry to come so late, Ms. Camden. I need to ask you some questions about Jordan King, also known as Jordan Bleu," Brice said, shoving Jordan's picture toward Dominique. Dominique looked down at the picture and cringed as if she had seen the devil himself. She wrapped her arms around her waist and cleared her desert-dry throat.

"How did you know I was here?" Dominique's voice cracked.

"I tracked you through My House . . . your history," Brice informed her.

Dominique swallowed the lump in her throat. "We can't speak here. My husband will be home soon and he doesn't . . . well, he . . ." Dominique started.

"Wherever you want to go is fine with me. But I desperately need your help," Brice said with emotion.

"I'm sorry, Detective. I can't help you. I don't know anything about Jordan Bleu. My dealings with him have long since been over," Dominique said, stepping back with her hand on the door.

"Please. You may be my only hope right now," Brice pleaded, placing his foot between the door and the frame.

"You have to find someone else to help you. Maybe Casey Pete . . . She is . . . she and Jordan are . . . Like I said, Detective. I wish I could help you but I just can't," Dominique said, her entire body feeling numb. Dominique wasn't ready to complete her journey through the past, especially not with this stranger.

"You should think about saving another girl like yourself," Brice said, lowering his head as she slammed the door in his face.

Dominique turned her back to the door and slid down to the floor. She began sobbing. "When I got clean and got married and moved into the big house it was all supposed to be better," she sobbed, speaking out loud to God. She didn't know why she couldn't just speak to the man and purge herself of her past sins once and for all.

Chapter Ten

Lies and Betrayal

"I can't believe this niggah left me out here," Dominique mumbled under her breath as she stormed toward her building. Jordan had not come to pick her up from work like he usually did. "What if a muthafucka had decided to go crazy on my ass? I would've been left for dead. Bastard . . . can't believe his spiteful ass," she continued her rant.

Last night Dominique and Jordan had argued over Casey's pitiful earnings. Dominique had come to Casey's defense since Jordan had gotten in Casey's face about how naive she'd been for only accepting $200 from one of their wealthier clients. Jordan was always on them about bringing in more money. Dominique wasn't afraid to voice her opinion to Jordan, but when he looked like he was about to strike Casey, she'd jumped in the line of fire. She knew how violent Jordan could become.

Jordan had changed from the days when it was just the two of them. He had become more aggressive and had even gotten physically violent with her on a few occasions. Dominique told herself she would stay with Jordan for a little while longer just for the protection he provided when she was out on the street. Given what happened to her the one time she tried to turn a trick on her own, Dominique told herself that as soon as she could figure out a way around his crazy ass, she would take Casey and run. The two of them could open up their own high-class escort service and Dominique could get her ass off the streets. Although Dominique knew Casey didn't deal with the grimy johns she dealt with, she worried about her anyway.

Over time, the two had become best friends. Dominique leaned on Casey for moral support when she missed her mother and Casey did the same. They reminisced with each other about the good times in their childhoods but also helped each other through the rough times.

Dominique rushed her last trick and raced home to see how much Casey had banked for the night. Casey usually brought in big bucks because of the type of clients she dealt with—rich ones. That's why when Jordan had complained about the one time Casey's take was low, Dominique jumped into it.

Dominique had showed Casey the trick of taking out her cut first, before giving anything over to Jordan. Dominique snatched off her heels before she began the task of climbing the stairs to the apartment she now shared with Jordan and Casey. With her key already in hand, she unlocked the door and rushed inside.

The apartment was dark and Jordan and Casey were nowhere in sight. As Dominique clicked on some lights, she could hear muffled voices. Inching around the living room, she realized that the noise was coming from the bedroom. Dominique stood by the bedroom door with every nerve ending on her body alert. She listened to the moans and sounds of skin slapping together. She recognized Casey's voice and Jordan's moans.

The sounds assailed the inside of her ears and caused her heart to pound. How dare they fuck in her house?

Dominique flexed her jaw at their audacity. She could envision Jordan and Casey's bodies tangled together, fitted one atop the other like the keys of a piano—ebony and ivory. Dominique swallowed the lump that was forming in the back of her throat, her instincts telling her to knock down the door and start whipping some ass, but her feet were somehow rooted to the floor. Although Dominique didn't want to hear it, she had to listen. Just for assurance. A feeling of betrayal strangled Dominique as she heard Casey moan in ecstasy.

Jordan had been hers for years. Although Dominique and Jordan had agreed years ago after the first time they had sex that they were better off as "homie-lover-friends," Dominique still felt that aside from the occasional worker sucking him off, he belonged to her. It should have been pretty clear to Casey that he was off limits, since Dominique was the one responsible for converting Casey from a backward know-nothing to a high-priced call girl for the rich and famous. Dominique had been with her every step of the way, teaching her all the tricks of the trade. Once Casey had gotten the swing of things, Jordan had instructed Dominique to stop going on the dates with Casey. Of course, this was only after some prejudiced-ass clients complained about Dominique's "ghetto girl" appearance.

Dominique had taken a lot of shit from Jordan for Casey's sake. Dominique bit her bottom lip and started slamming things, making noises loud enough to alert Jordan and Casey that she was home. It didn't seem to work. Their moans drifted through the door, making it harder for Dominique to ignore. She couldn't hold back her tears anymore. "He ain't gettin' this fucking money I worked for all night just to feed his little princess," Dominique grumbled, snatching Jordan's prized car keys and storming out the door.

Dominique often thought about going into business for herself; but each time she considered it, she thought of Gordo and the few other crazy johns she had encountered and immediately discarded the idea. Jordan had always offered her protection, but tonight told a different story. What if she got caught up in a bad situation tonight? How could he have possibly reached her in time? There were some pretty sick fucks out there.

Dominique drove all the way up to Harlem without getting stopped by any cops. Over the years she had learned to drive, but never bothered to get her license. She unloaded the bags of groceries she had picked up and entered the familiar building. When she knocked on the apartment door, she set the bags down knowing it would take a while. When Mama Grady finally opened the door and flashed her beautiful smile, it seemed like all of Dominique's problems just faded away. Dominique had never forgotten Mama Grady and anytime she got a chance to visit, in between working, she did. It was the one place she could escape to that even Jordan didn't know about.

"Hi, baby!" Mama Grady greeted, her voice rippled and fluid like water in a stream.

"I got you some fruit," Dominique said, entering with a fake smile plastered on her face. Anytime she had something on her mind, she knew Mama Grady would make it all right.

"Well, thank you, baby. Gon' put them in the Frigidaire and set down for something to eat," Mama Grady instructed.

"I'm not even hungry. I just came by to say hi," Dominique lied. She'd come by for that motherly comfort she was desperately lacking.

"Food can always turn a frown upside down," Mama Grady laughed, her ample bosom shaking like a bowl of Jell-O.

"Mama Grady, you ever been in love with somebody who didn't love you back?" Dominique asked, looking down at the speckles on the old Formica table.

"Why, chile, yes. When I was a girl in South Carolina, I loved this boy. *Ew-wee!* He was fine as wine but he loved my friend. Oh, I was so heartbroken that I stopped speaking to them but then—" Mama Grady started.

"Me too!" Dominique interjected, her face lighting up. "Dag, you always know what's up," Dominique whispered, wishing she were her real "mama."

"Listen, girl. Don't you worry about loving no man. You needs to learn to love yourself and then you gon' find a man who will love you just the same. A man knows when you don't have no love for yourself, so they treat you accordingly. When you love yourself, you give off a glow that tells the no-good ones to back on up," Mama Grady consoled, hugging Dominique tight.

Dominique felt warm inside. "I'll take some food," Dominique said, smiling, needing to change the subject. It was either that or admit to Mama Grady that she did not know how to love herself because no one had ever loved her before, except maybe her own mama. But that was a lifetime ago.

When Sharon arrived home, Dominique knew it was time to leave. It had been years since she first met Mama Grady and no matter how nice Dominique treated Mama Grady, Sharon still did not accept their relationship. Sometimes Dominique told herself that Sharon was just jealous.

"You here again?" Sharon snorted, giving Dominique a once-over.

Dominique's eyes hooded over. Frankly, she was tired of Sharon's shit. "I was being leaving," Dominique assured her, just as snide. "Bye, Mama Grady. I will see you soon," Dominique said, giving Mama Grady her customary hug.

When Dominique got to the door, Sharon grabbed her by the arm.

"I know what you do for a living—I seen you. Don't be bringing your dirty sex and diseases around my mama," Sharon said through gritted teeth.

A chill shot up Dominique's spine as she wrestled her arm away from Sharon. "Don't you worry about what *I* do. At least I talk to your mama and treat her like somebody. Which is more than you can say, *Ms. Social Security Check Thief*," Dominique retorted, snatching open the door.

"Don't let me see you over here no more or I will call the cops and tell 'em what you do!" Sharon threatened as Dominique walked to her car.

Mama Grady's words about loving herself; Sharon's threats; and Casey and Jordan's betrayal swirled around her head like a tornado. She slammed her hands on the steering wheel. Lately, even the purple haze couldn't provide her with the escape that she needed.

Dominique had heard from one of the girls in the stable that black tar was the shit. It could be smoked and have the same potency as shooting up, the girl had told her. Dominique had vowed not to dabble with the hardcore shit because she'd seen its devastating effects. But the more she worked, the harder it became to deal with reality. She always felt men's hands touching her body. Even when she showered, Dominique felt like she could not get the smell of semen or saliva off. The raw scent of sex stayed with her and it was slowly driving her mad.

Dominique unfolded the foil wrapper with the drug inside. She looked at the little black lump that she had harbored in her bag for over two weeks. She'd been contemplating taking it, but hadn't been courageous enough to take the final step. This time, she went for it. The girl had instructed Dominique to put the lump in her weed bong and just light up the bottom. Dominique followed the instructions to the letter and found a place that she could go where she felt no pain.

Casey had become a new woman since being rescued from the streets. She walked with an air of confidence and always sold sex to the highest bidder. For Casey, it was the ultimate way to tell the prophet to go fuck himself. Everything she had learned as a child didn't matter. This was her life now.

Dominique had really gone out of her way to break Casey in to the life—she'd even showed her how to tongue kiss properly before her first real date. Casey and Dominique shopped, laughed and cried together. She confided in Dominique about everything, except her "thing" with Jordan. She was afraid it might make Dominique jealous. Casey had noticed that Dominique could be very territorial when it came to Jordan. Uncomfortable with keeping secrets from her friend, Casey told herself that she would just have to find the right time to tell Dominique.

When Dominique arrived back at the apartment, Jordan was furious. "Where the fuck you been with my car?" he boomed.

"Out," Dominique said dryly, tossing his keys at him.

"What the fuck you mean, 'out'? If you was going out, why the fuck you took my car? You were supposed to be working anyway!" Jordan ranted, his black face turning almost purple.

"Yeah, I'm supposed to be working while the fucking great white hope entertains you, right?" Dominique spat.

"Stop being fuckin' jealous and step up your game!" Jordan barked, his vindictive words like a slap in the face.

Casey came sauntering out of the bedroom to investigate

the ruckus. She wore a sheer bathrobe, her golden locks hanging down on either side of her neck just enough to cover her nipples. She looked like a movie star.

Dominique sucked her teeth. "This bitch," Dominique muttered under her breath.

Casey didn't say anything. The tension in the room was palpable and Casey thought if she opened her mouth things might implode.

"Yo, Diamond, for real. You better check yourself before you wreck yourself. A niggah ain't in the mood for your shenanigans," Jordan warned.

"Fuck you, you fuckin' traitor. I was the one there for you when C-Lo played your little punk ass. You ain't nuthin' but a bitch-ass niggah," Dominique replied, letting hurt dictate her words and cloud her judgment. Dominique rolled her eyes and turned her back on Jordan. She suddenly felt a rush of wind, then a sharp pain like her neck was being yanked from her body. Jordan grabbed a handful of her weave and dragged her backward. Dominique yelped in pain.

"Don't ever fuckin' disrespect me. I made you and I own you," Jordan growled, his hot breath burning her face like a torch. Shocked, Dominique was incapable of speech. Jordan was out of control again and she knew just how far he could go. He unraveled his hand from her hair and shoved her to the ground. Dominique landed on her knees, prostrate in front of him, as if to beg for mercy.

"Now get the fuck up and give me my money!" Jordan spat. Casey looked on helplessly, unable to decide whether her allegiance lay with her lover or friend.

Two weeks had passed since Jordan and Dominique's dust-up. The two went through the days avoiding each other.

Some nights he would pick Dominique up to assure her of his protection, but other nights he left her to fend for herself. Casey felt caught in the middle of the feud. Dominique barely spoke to her anymore, although Casey had tried several times to apologize for whatever she had done to upset her friend.

It was a Saturday morning and Casey had just returned to the apartment from one of her high-class "dates." Dominique sat at the kitchen table sipping tea. The night before, she had been out in the cold rain for so long that she felt like ice chips had frosted to her bones and she would be defrosting for days.

"Diamond, I got exciting news!" Casey said, rushing over to the table where Dominique sat. Dominique looked up at her "friend" with disgust. "I know you've been mad at me, but look . . . look at this," Casey said, tossing a business card down on the table. *Mikey Cuntmore, Cuntmore Productions.*

"And?" Dominique said, unenthused.

"My client from last night works with this guy and he could make us movie stars," Casey said excitedly.

"I'm not interested," Dominique grumbled.

"C'mon, Diamond . . . we can be big stars," Casey pleaded.

"You are already a big star," Dominique said enviously. Dominique sucked her teeth and stood up to leave. She needed to get her fix of heroin, which she now used on a regular basis. The monkey was slowly crawling onto her back. Dominique started walking away, but Casey continued talking anyway.

"Just consider it," Casey yelled at Dominique's back. Casey threw the card down on the table and flopped into a nearby chair. It was times like these that she wished she could have pursued her dreams of becoming a ballerina.

Jordan rushed into the apartment in a huff. He raced into the bedroom he now shared with Casey to get his weapon from his safe.

"Diamond!" he called out. Casey tried to walk over to him to give him the good news, but he brushed past her like she was invisible. "Diamond!" Jordan called out again, banging on the other bedroom door.

"Yeah, Jordan," Dominique answered, snatching the door open, her face twisted up in disgust.

"We need to go to East New York right now! There's a problem," Jordan huffed.

"A problem with what? You haven't taken me to collect in a minute," Dominique said, looking at him suspiciously. All of a sudden he wanted her help?

"I need you to talk to one of these bitches. She bugging right now," Jordan panted, sweat dripping down his temples. "Get dressed and let's go," Jordan said with finality. Dominique mumbled and did as she was told. She didn't want to hear his mouth. Besides, she had just gotten her mind right with a little help from her new best friend—heroin.

"Can I go?" Casey asked, like they were going to an amusement park. Dominique looked at her like she was crazy. Casey was still a bit of a lost child.

When they arrived at the apartment on Stanley Avenue where Jordan kept his girls, he rushed out of the car with the urgency of somebody going to save a dying friend. Dominique and Casey were right on his heels. Once they were inside, Jordan rushed toward one of the bedrooms. "Where is she?!" he called out. Several girls pointed, their eyes wide with fear. "Get the fuck out on the streets! I want everybody the fuck up outta here!" he screamed.

Jordan opened another bedroom door to find the girl sitting on a dirty mattress that had no sheets. She was naked and trembling. A tall, skinny teenage boy stood in front of her, a silver .22-caliber revolver tucked in the front of his pants. Jordan had hired two ruthless teenage boys to ensure that his girls were out on the streets when they were supposed to be and that they didn't try anything funny at the apartment. The boy had kept the little shivering girl there long enough for Jordan to get there.

"So what's the problem now?" Jordan asked, sucking in his bottom lip.

"She said she was going back home. Then I heard the ho tell one of the other girls that she would be sending the cops back to get us all locked the fuck up," the boy explained. Hearing the news, Jordan popped open his Mylanta and took a long swig. He was circling like an animal ready to attack.

"A'ight, I got this from here. I want everybody up outta here until I can sort this shit out," Jordan said, dismissing the boy.

"Yo, niggah, I'm telling you, I can take care her for you," the boy assured, wanting to get on Jordan's good side.

"Nah, dude, she wanna go home . . . I'ma let her ass go home. Now get the fuck out," Jordan ordered. The boy bopped out of the room, trying hard to keep up his tough-guy demeanor. Jordan couldn't risk that kid running his mouth on the streets to win brownie points with his little cronies. He had to take care of this shit himself.

Jordan walked over to the little girl. She looked up at him with eyes that resembled a *Precious Moments* figurine.

"So you goin' home all of a sudden? You wasn't saying that shit when you was enjoying the wining and dining, right?" Jordan grabbed the girl by the neck and positioned her face so that she would have to look him in the eye. Dominique knew that all the little girl had to do was say that she would work for her daddy forever and Jordan probably would've been satisfied. But no, the little girl kept insisting that she wanted to go home.

Dominique stepped up from behind Jordan, her eyebrows

furrowed. Most of the girls in the apartment were new and very young. Dominique squinted her eyes into little dashes and shook her head from left to right. Jordan had violated the one rule Dominique asked him not to—no fucking with little girls. Disgusted,

Dominique stormed out of the room.

As Dominique headed for the door of the apartment, she heard loud bangs and crashes coming from the room. Jordan's voice could be heard rising and falling like booms of thunder, then the girl's screams resounded like high keening notes that cut the air into almost suffocating slices. Dominique paced outside of the room while Casey bit the acrylic off of her nail tips. Dominique decided she had to stop Jordan's crazy tirade before it was too late. If he kept it up much longer, he would definitely catch an attempted murder charge.

Dominique rushed through the doorway of the bedroom, Casey fast on her heels. Casey hated violence, having witnessed numerous public beatings as a child on the compound.

"Jordan, I think—" Dominique started, but stopped as soon as she took in the scene. The smell of fresh blood was so potent she could taste it on her tongue. Jordan was stomping the little girl in the chest. His eyes were flashing red and his nostrils flared. He was clearly in another place. Dominique had never seen him like this before. She looked at the heap of flesh that was once a little girl and then back at the crazed maniac who had done this to her. Dominique could hear her own heart beating in her ears.

"Jordan, what did you do?" Dominique screamed, placing her hand over her mouth as she looked down at the bloody mess that was once the little girl's face.

"Oh, my God! She is not breathing!" Casey screamed, jumping up and down in a panic.

"Everybody just shut the fuck up and calm down!" Jordan

barked, pacing the floor a few feet away from the girl's limp body. Jordan reached in his back pocket to get his relief. He took a gulp of his third bottle of Mylanta for the day and continued to pace.

With her hands trembling fiercely, Dominique bent down and touched the girl's neck. "She's dead, Jordan! You fuckin' beat her to death!" Dominique screamed, placing her hands on both sides of her head, pulling her hair.

"Well, we just gon' have to get rid of a body then. Y'all stood here and watched, which makes y'all accessories to murder," Jordan replied menacingly, stepping closer to Dominique and Casey, flashing the gun that was stuffed in his waistband.

Jordan forced Dominique and Casey to help him roll the little girl up in a comforter and carry her to his car. Dominique moved like a zombie and Casey sobbed loudly as they did the deed. Jordan went outside and surveyed the block, looking around nervously to make sure no one would take notice.

Once they had the body in the backseat, Dominique climbed in the backseat, cradling the swaddled girl. She touched the dead girl's hair, reminded of the last time she'd encountered death.

"This was a fucking baby, Jordan," Dominique sobbed. Casey popped two pills in her mouth and swallowed them without anything to drink. Jordan realized he would be leaving one of his main sources of income behind. Their new secret formed a solid barrier between them like the Great Wall of China. They could never come back to that apartment again.

In the weeks following the murder, the television and newspaper reports sent Dominique further and further into depression. Dominique kept envisioning dumping the poor little girl's body in an alley behind a bodega in the thick of the night. As a result, she became increasingly dependent on her drugs. The heroin addiction had become a bit expensive, so Dominique took to smoking weed laced with crack cocaine. When she had the money, heroin was always her first choice.

Although Dominique wasn't physically showing the effects of the deadly medicine, mentally she was a shell of a person. Casey's nerves were also on edge. She cried constantly, forcing Jordan to obtain more illegal prescription pills to calm her down. Neither girl could sleep at night, as they were both haunted by visions of the girl.

One night while Dominique lay tossing and turning, Jordan entered her bedroom.

"Diamond," he called out, but she was already awake. She stared at him

blankly. "I got an idea that can make us some money and you won't have to go back on the stroll," Jordan offered. Dominique sat up at attention—more money meant more drugs. "Casey got the number of a movie producer . . ."Jordan started. Dominique rolled her eyes and lay back down. "Diamond, look, I'm sorry about everything, a'ight? But you can't act like a baby now. We all need to do this. You wanna grow old selling your shit on the streets?" Jordan asked.

"What's the difference?" Dominique asked.

"Exactly! So why not be famous for it?" Jordan's face lit up with possibility. Dominique had never thought of it like that. She did have an expensive habit to feed. "What do we have to do?" Dominique asked resignedly.

Jordan was happier than Dominique had seen him in a long while. He was dressed up in a grey Sean Jean business suit and wing tip shoes. He told Dominique and Casey to wear their best form-fitting dresses. Dominique donned an all-black, one-shoulder spandex dress with black fishnet stockings, and Casey wore a tight, red, ruche-front, satin mini with no stockings. When they were all ready, Dominique thought they looked like an entourage of pimp and hoes. Dominique commented on the fact and they all shared an easy laugh. It was the first time in a while that the atmosphere didn't crackle with tension.

They rode to Manhattan in style—Jordan had recently purchased a new BMW. Dominique ran a thousand possible scenarios through her mind about what she would do and where she would go if she made it big. First thing, she would make sure Mama Grady was taken care of with a new house and servants who would wait on her hand and foot. Then Dominique would buy herself a house away from the big city, near a beach with clear blue water. Most importantly, she would put away enough money that she could focus on getting an education.

When they arrived on West Fifty-seventh Street, Dominique looked around in awe. Mikey Cuntmore's office and studio were located amid some of the richest properties in New York. Dominique would've never guessed it. Jordan parked the car and they all took the parking lot elevator to the sixth floor. Mikey's office had beautiful glass doors and an intercom system.

"Looks nice!" Casey whispered to Dominique excitedly.

"I hope it pays as nice as it looks," Dominique replied.

"Don't mention money when we get in there," Jordan instructed just before they were buzzed in.

"Jordan Bleu is it?" asked a young man who looked like he could be a college intern.

"Yeah, yeah, that's me," Jordan said, flashing his pearly white teeth.

"I'm Dave, Mikey's assistant," the man said, looking at his occasional fuck-buddy, Casey.

"Pleased to meet you," Jordan replied, trying his best to bring back the college-graduate demeanor that he'd buried so long ago for the street-dude façade he kept up with these days.

They all followed Dave down a long hallway to a huge conference room with a long, glass-top table and several high-back, leather swivel chairs. Inside were large framed posters of some of the most beautiful naked women Domnique had ever seen. Dominique didn't know if it was airbrushing or surgery, but those bitches were hot.

Dave noticed the girls ogling the pictures. "Yes, these are some of our girls. Most are the biggest stars in the industry. Mikey is amazing," Dave said proudly.

"Well, we are ready to rock," Jordan interjected, rubbing his hands together to calm his nerves.

"Ready to rock . . . I like that," a voice boomed from behind. They all jumped, turning their attention toward the door.

"This is the man himself, Mikey Cuntmore," Dave introduced, stepping aside. Jordan rushed toward Mikey like he was the Dalai Lama, grabbing his hand for a shake. Mikey took his hand back and rubbed it on his pants leg as if Jordan had a disease.

Dominique gave Mikey the once-over. He was about 400 pounds, with three chins and a stomach that bulged unhealthily over his belt buckle. His hair was a slick mess of grease and mousse. He had attempted to take the six strands he had at the top and comb them over the ever-present bald spot in the middle—but had failed miserably. He smelled of Old Spice and cigarettes. Dominique shuddered, not getting a good vibe from the dude. He reminded her of some of her less-than-pleasant johns.

"Let's get started . . . Time is money in my business," Mikey informed. Everyone took their seats. Mikey asked for Casey to do a 360, then he began his interrogation.

"She on any drugs?"

"Nah, she's clean," Jordan answered.

"What's her measurements?"

"Thirty-two; twenty-six; thirty-two," Jordan replied.

"Has she ever had the clap?"

"She grew up a Mormon . . . She's clean," Jordan answered.

They kept this up for about ten minutes, talking about Casey as if she were not there.

"Take it off, baby. I need to see the merchandise and get some test shots," Mikey said, licking his lips. Casey raised her eyebrows and looked at Jordan helplessly. She didn't know she would have to undress in front of everyone—although that's what porn was all about.

Casey slowly peeled off her clothes, feeling like she was taking off layers of her skin until she was down to bones.

"Come over here," Mikey instructed, with a yellow-toothed grin. Casey slowly ambled over to where he sat. She shrank back when he reached out to touch her breast.

"Pretty nice," he said, squeezing one of her breasts. "Turn around," Mikey instructed, breathing hard. Casey closed her eyes and turned. Mikey squeezed one of her ass cheeks and then slapped it. Casey jumped. What was he going to do next? Check her teeth like the farmers did when selecting good livestock?

"She's good," Mikey said, motioning to Dave. Dave slid some paperwork toward Jordan. Casey gathered up her clothes and ran out of the room. Dominique was next up. She had slipped out while Casey was being poked, prodded and slapped. She returned so high and mellow, she didn't take offense to his questions or instructions. When she bent over to show him the goods, she had a big smile plastered on her face. They wanted acting; she'd give them acting. Mikey was done with her in less than five minutes.

"I like the white girl. I'm not so sure the black girl is marketable. She got some scars that people just don't wanna see," Mikey told Jordan.

"Nah, she is hot. She ain't got nothin' a little makeup can't fix. They could be a good mix—vanilla and chocolate," Jordan said, trying to push for a package deal.

"I don't know. I'll try it for the first run," Mikey said skeptically. "They need names," he said. Jordan had already thought of that angle. He'd spent a couple of days reviewing names of the biggest porno stars and he came up with Denver Peaks for Casey and Diamond Tiara for Dominique. Mikey liked the names. Jordan served as Casey and Dominique's agent, so he conducted all of the monetary negotiations. Mikey offered Jordan $10,000 for their first movie. If it did well, the next deal would be much more lucrative.

Casey's hand trembled as she tossed in her mouth four Vicodens that Jordan had given her. She prayed that they would take effect quickly. The movie set was crowded. Casey didn't know how she could perform with all of these people watching, although it wouldn't be the first time.

On the night of her wedding at the compound, the prophet and several of his main elders had watched Casey lose her virginity to ensure that the wedding had been consummated. Casey had lain on the clean, flowered sheets like a sacrificial lamb. Several men stood at the foot of the bed, while the prophet doled out instructions. Her vision was blurred from all of the tears. She felt the bed dip and bow as Samson climbed onto it. Closing her eyes tightly, Casey began to sob so hard she felt like the veins in her temple would burst.

"Shhhh," Samson hushed her, forcing her handsewn nightgown over her hips.

"Please don't!" Casey begged.

"It's God's order," the prophet intoned. Samson tried several times to get her to submit, but Casey continued to resist. Her small frame was a challenge even for Samson's strength. It had taken him several hours to enter her body. Casey screamed when he finally penetrated her. Ignoring her outrage, he continued to move in her until the elders were all satisfied that God had blessed the marriage.

Casey blinked away the memories and smiled, feeling the effects of the new shit Jordan had given her begin to "take the edge off." Casey was ready to get this show started. She frowned, noticing that Dominique was taking forever in the bathroom to get ready.

"You ready to be a star?" Jordan asked her. Casey had a lazy grin on her face. When she was like this, it was anything goes. Jordan walked back to the bathroom door behind the set. "Yo, Diamond! What's up?" Jordan called out, hitting the door with two knuckles.

"I'm coming!" Dominique hollered back. She came stumbling out of the bathroom, her eyes vacant.

"Let's get this show on the road . . . Mikey is waiting," Jordan said eagerly.

Dominique and Casey moved around each other stiffly, like robots. They were doing scenes for their movie debut and the first scene was going to be of them . . . together.

"Denver, lay back and turn your face toward camera A," Mikey instructed. "Diamond, I want your head between her legs. Stick your tongue out and put it up against her clit," Mikey continued.

Dominique gulped hard. She had never even considered lesbian sex before. With money on her mind, Dominique closed her eyes and buried her face between Casey's legs, licking her clitoris like she'd done it a hundred times before. Dominique felt like she'd suffocate, taking in the scent of Casey's natural musk and the strong perfume she'd doused herself with.

"Casey, I need sound, motion. You love this, act like it," Mikey called out. Casey began to moan on cue, gyrating her hips slightly. Casey closed her eyes, her body violating her as her vagina became soaking wet against her will. Dominique's knees began to burn from being on them too long. She could feel the heat of the camera on her ass cheeks, then the hands of some of Mikey's assistants on either side, spreading her flesh apart. They were filming her ass too. Dominique put her feelings of degradation aside. She mentally put herself at Mama Grady's table, the only place she could think of that offered her comfort.

Jordan roved the set like a lion protecting his pride. His dick was as hard as a roll of quarters. He didn't really think this would turn him on. Watching Dominique's cocoa skin up against Casey's pale skin had sent heated sparks down Jordan's legs. He wanted to reach into his pants and just jerk off right there.

Casey and Dominique did several more takes before Mikey had enough footage for the movie. Back in the changing room, Dominique and Casey did not speak or make eye contact.

Within two months, Casey and Dominique had made four more movies together. All of them were a hit in the industry. They were blowing up on the porn scene. There had even been a one-page article in *Penthouse* magazine describing them as "the new ebony and ivory sensation." Neither of them needed to turn tricks any longer.

"Diamond! Cas!" Jordan called out. Casey came out of the

bedroom rubbing her eyes and Dominique was locked up in the bathroom as usual.

"Yo, I just found out the new movie is a bigger hit! They love that chocolate and vanilla girl-on-girl shit," Jordan said excitedly.

"Yay!" Casey said, giggling like she did when she was high.

Dominique finally came out of her new hiding spot, her pupils dilated and sweat sprinkled over her forehead. "What's good?" she asked.

Jordan looked at her strangely.

"The movie is blowing up. They want us to come to L.A. to meet a new producer . . . an even bigger name," Jordan told her.

"Awww," Dominique belted out, clapping her hands together. "Show me the money!" she sang.

Jordan had yet to give either of them their real share of the money. He had made himself their "agent" so he had cashed all the checks.

"When I get paid, you'll get paid," Jordan promised. In the meantime, he gave them just enough to keep them quiet and to feed their growing habits.

They headed to L.A. with big dreams on their minds. Mikey had referred them to one of his West Coast affiliates who were looking for raw, clean talent like Casey. He hadn't mentioned anything about Dominique.

Chapter Eleven

Doing the Right Thing

"There is now a forty thousand-dollar reward offered for any information regarding Ciara Simpson—the missing sister of heroic NYPD detective Brice Simpson. Detective Simpson spoke to reporters earlier today: "My sister is not a runaway. She is a good student and a good girl. I am asking whoever has her to release her. We are not looking to harm you. All we want is for Ciara to come home." Here is a picture of Ciara Simpson. She was last seen wearing blue jeans, blue and white Nike sneakers and a black hooded jacket. Detective Simpson and the NYPD have launched a massive search for the girl who never returned from school a week ago. They are asking anyone with information to call 1-800-CRIMESTOPPERS. You can remain anonymous."

Casey was about to throw her last few things into her suitcase when the story on the news caught her attention. She dropped her bottle of perfume, sending it crashing to the floor when the picture of the missing girl flashed on the screen. "Oh my God," Casey gasped. She scrambled out of her bedroom and ran over to her dining room table. She began frantically sifting through the piles of junk mail she had let accumulate since she'd been home from the hospital. "Dammit!" she cursed when she couldn't find the Polaroid test shots Jordan had left behind.

Casey sat at the table and rummaged through the piles of papers, shaking each piece of mail out. Finally, something fell to the floor. Casey exhaled. Casey lifted up the photograph to examine it, her heart hammering against her sternum. With her hands trembling, she raced over to get her cell phone. After her hospital stay, Casey had a new telephone number added to her contacts list. Casey frantically scrolled through her list and located the number of the only person who always knew the answers—her best friend, Diamond.

"Oh, Alton. Yes, Alton," Dominique panted out, pretend-ing to love it. She stared up at the ceiling, praying this torture would be over soon. She bit into her lip to deal with the surges of pain—her ribs still ached from being only partially healed, and her vagina was desert dry so the friction from each movement felt like acid burns. Alton pumped on top of her like a horny dog. He had his face buried in the skin of her neck as he panted with labored breaths, sweat beads dripping onto her chest. Lately, his sex drive had been in overdrive and Dominique knew that if she didn't submit there would be consequences.

When he was done, he did his usual routine. He jumped up and raced into their master bathroom. He turned the spigot in the shower as hot as it could go and then scrubbed himself for the next half hour. Alton had made her feel like she was a dirty disease each time they had made love. It bothered her at first, but after almost a year of marriage, she had learned to ignore it.

Dominique had not been able to concentrate on much since the visit from the detective. Although she had treated him horribly, he had stuck his card in the door before he left. Dominique had picked it up several times, but it wasn't because she wanted to give him any history about Jordan or agree to help his cause. She rubbed her fingers over his embossed name and pictured his face. She wondered if he were her husband, what life would be like. Dominique felt ashamed that she could remember in vivid detail his smooth caramel skin, his sleepy light brown eyes and his soothing, even baritone.

Dominique regretted that she hadn't been able to give him the information he was seeking. She had been honest with him when she said she did not know where Jordan was right now. Dominique had only seen him the one time at the hospital in the last year. She had not been ready to tell the detective anything about herself, for fear that it might become public knowledge. After all the program had taught her, it still was not enough to keep her past in the past.

Dominique turned over on her side and noticed from across the room that the light on her cell phone was flashing. She had purposely switched it to silent mode. Given her recent contact with the detective, Casey and even that bastard Jordan, Dominique couldn't take a chance with them calling while Alton was home. Dominique threw her legs over the side of the bed and pulled on her sweat pants. She still had on her T-shirt and bra; Alton never let her get fully naked when they made love. Dominique padded over to her dresser and picked up the phone. The missed calls screen was full. Dominique scrolled through the calls and they were all from Casey. *Maybe she is calling to tell me she won't tell everything in her tell-all interview.* Dominique certainly hoped that was the case. Dominique quickly threw her cell phone into her underwear drawer as the shower spigot turned off. She would call Casey back when she got a chance. If she got a chance.

***

"Did you take the pills that I gave you, baby girl?" Jordan asked. The girl giggled and shook her head. "Good girl," Jordan said, stroking her beautiful, long hair.

"Well, I guess this is as good a payback as it could be. I would rather have white but a black girl for a kiddie porn flick will do," Mikey said as he walked over to Jordan and his new prospect. The little girl was butt naked—her body resembling that of a woman with thirty-six C-cup breasts; round hips; and her butt so round and perfect Jordan had named it "the cherry."

"You stooped to a new low, Jordan Bleu, but I like it," Mikey said, grinning like the Cheshire Cat. The set was low budget—a bed, a few lights and one camera. Kiddie porn perverts didn't need any frills; they got off just knowing there was a child involved in a lewd act.

"You say she is barely sixteen? These perv hounds are gonna love her," he continued.

Mikey wasn't investing any more big dollars in Jordan until he recouped what he had lost from the Denver Peaks Fuck Fest fiasco. Mikey had to admit to himself, Jordan came through rather quickly with a solution. If he hadn't, Mikey had been ready to send his mafia goon friends after Jordan.

"I'm cold," the girl said, laughing again, the drugs surging through her system.

"You're going to be hot in a minute," Jordan said. He pulled his shirt over his head and began taking off his jeans. Jordan had decided that he was going to be the star of this show. When the movie sold on the underground, he would be the one reaping all of the benefits.

"Get on your knees and put your head right here baby girl," Jordan said, pointing and positioning her in front of his waist. He pulled a black ski mask over his face so only his eyes were clear to the camera. Mikey smiled wickedly and clicked on his camera while his assistant started snapping photos.

***

Once Brice learned about Jordan's real history, he took to the media and to the streets. He wasn't waiting around for the NYPD missing persons squad to do shit for him. Brice knew how they operated, especially when they figured a girl was just a sixteen-year-old runaway.

"She's my fucking sister!" Brice screamed, banging the desk in front of where he stood.

"I don't give a fuck! You don't go to the media unless you have clearance from the department!" Sergeant Curruthers barked, his pale face turning bright pink.

"Sarg, I have investigated these fucking runaway cases for years and I never went to the media. I mean, what makes this case so special? I understand she's a cop's sister, but they run away, too," D'Guilio interjected.

Brice didn't know what the fuck he was even doing in the meeting. "What, muthafucka? She is not a fuckin' runaway! She is a missing fuckin' person! Somebody took her off the street!" Brice barked, the vein in his neck pulsing fiercely against his skin.

"Simpson . . . there are ways to handle this. It's a conflict of interest for you to be involved. You are too emotional. Missing persons is handling it," Sergeant Curruthers said. Brice bit down into his jaw.

"Do you have an answer for me to give my mother? Huh? She wants to know why her fuckin' son is a hero cop but can't find his own goddamned sister!" Brice said, rocking on his heels. Sergeant Curruthers exhaled wearily.

"I want the fuckin' commissioner himself to tell me I can't help with the search for my sister. I want you bastards to put yourself in my shoes. If it were one of your precious daughters that was missing . . ." Brice continued, pointing a finger in Sergeant Curruthers' face. He was not backing down.

"I've had enough of this sideshow bullshit. A runaway is a fucking runaway any way you slice it," D'Guilio said, a slick smile on his face.

Suddenly, Brice felt like the walls were closing in on him. The corners of his eyes grew black, and he couldn't see anything in his peripheral vision. Brice whirled around, an unknown force moving him, and punched D'Guilio in his nose. Blood spurted onto Brice's suit. D'Guilio fell to the floor.

Brice jumped on top of D'Guilio and began hammering him in the head and face with his fists. Sergeant Curruthers scrambled from behind his desk and grabbed the back of Brice's suit jacket in an attempt to pull Brice off of D'Guilio. Sergeant Curruthers was no match for Brice's brute strength. Brice bucked like the Incredible Hulk, sending Sergeant Curruthers stumbling backward.

"Help in here!" Sergeant Curruthers screamed out.

The door to the sergeant's office suddenly burst open and several detectives swarmed in and descended on the heap of tangled arms and legs. They were able to pull Brice upright, but D'Guilio was already unconscious. Brice's chest heaved in and out with fury. His knuckles were a scraped, bloody mess. His clothes were stained with sweat and blood and the back of this jacket was ripped. With wide, wild eyes, he looked into the faces of his fellow detectives, all staring at him like he was a mad man. "Get a bus right now!" someone yelled from the group. One of the detectives ran to the phone to call in an ambulance for D'Guilio.

"Detective Simpson, you are suspended indefinitely. Hand over your gun and shield and get the fuck out of my precinct!" Sergeant Curruthers ordered, flexing his jaw so hard his head hurt.

***

Casey anxiously awaited Dominique's call. She kept looking at the pictures from the envelope that had been on her dining room table and then looking at the telephone. She did this incessantly for two hours until she built up the nerve to call CrimeStoppers. The representative on the phone made Casey feel as if she were lying about the information she provided. Casey grew frustrated with the twenty questions and slammed down the receiver. She needed some pills in her system if she was going to make it through the day. "Would she call? Oh, God, if you love me, let her call," Casey prayed, sharp pains ripping through her stomach. That always happened when her need kicked in. She had been trying to stay clean since her hospital stay, but it was a struggle every day. Today was the worst of all.

Anxiously pacing, Casey was jolted by the vibrating phone on the coffee table. Casey looked down at the screen and a feeling of relief washed over her. Casey remembered the detective's name from the news report and through Google had learned that he was promoted to the Brooklyn North Task Force.

Casey called a car service and headed to the address. Dominique had agreed to meet her there. Casey rocked her legs back and forth as the cab inched across the Brooklyn Bridge in traffic. She looked down at the pictures in her lap and hoped to God it was the right girl. Casey knew that Jordan was certainly capable of it. Besides that, she was feeling a bit vengeful.

At the precinct, Casey paid the car service driver and raced inside. She didn't know who to ask for help and she did not see Dominique. Finally, she spotted a sign that read 1-2-4 Room.

"Excuse me," Casey spoke to a middle-aged black woman behind an old rickety desk talking on the phone.

"If you came to file a complaint, sit down right there until I get off the phone," the woman said dryly.

"Um . . . no, I need to see—" Casey started, but was cut off.

"I'm on the phone," the woman chastised. Casey waited about twenty minutes before she realized the rude employee wasn't going to help her. She walked out into the main area and saw a fat man in uniform sitting behind a huge desk.

"Excuse me," Casey tried once more.

"Who let you over here?" the man barked.

"I just walked over," Casey explained, furrowing her eyebrows and not understanding what the big deal was. The man stood up and looked around.

"Officer Stackhouse, help this lady," the man directed.

"Okay, Sarg," the officer agreed, looking at Casey like she was out of place. "Ma'am, how can I help you?" the officer asked unenthusiastically.

"I'm looking for Detective Brice Simpson," Casey said. The officer's eyes opened a few inches wider.

"He is no longer here. Let me get someone else who can help you," he said, motioning Casey to follow him up a staircase. They came to a door that read detectives. Casey followed him inside.

"Hey, Detective Page, this lady says she needs to see Detective Simpson. Can you help her?" Detective Page took one look at Casey and knew right away who she was. Just then, Dominique stood up from a chair next to Detective Page's desk. She and Casey locked eyes. Casey stretched her thin lips into a smile.

"Sure can. Anything she needed from Simpson, she can get from me," Page said, walking over to Casey. He walked Casey over to where Dominique stood. "Have a seat," he offered.

Before Casey sat down, she grabbed Dominique's hand. The heat of their hands together sent an almost electric current to Casey's heart. "I have information about that missing girl from the TV," Casey said, already holding on to the pictures.

"So I understand both of you want to help," Detective Page said, examining the photos. He jumped up and ran over to a phone. He dialed a number. "Simp . . . I got some very important people you might want to meet," Detective Page whispered, his eyes darting around the room. "There are two of them and they think they can help you find your sister—alive," he continued, lowering his voice even more. Detective Page and Brice were old friends. They had completed the academy together. Detective Page didn't want to chance any of the other detectives getting wind of him giving Brice information.

Dominique and Casey did not speak a word. They just held onto to each other for dear life. They would do just what Brice had said—save another girl's life—with the hope that neither ended up dead.

Chapter Tweleve

Price of Fame

<u>*Los Angeles, California*</u>

The media lights flashed, temporarily blinding Dominique as she stood in Casey's shadow. She had a fake smile plastered to her heavily made-up face as the paparazzi and the most notable porn industry executives yelled questions. Casey stood at the podium, waving and smiling.

"Denver, this is your first solo project. How do you feel doing a film without Diamond?" a reporter for *Smut Magazine* screamed over the roar.

"Well, I'm happy to be doing the solo project, but I will definitely miss Diamond," Casey responded.

"Do you think your solo film will be better without Diamond?" another reporter asked.

"I'm ready to branch out. I want to give my fans what they deserve," Casey answered. Dominique stepped off the stage and ran out of the back door of the building. No one even noticed she was gone. Jordan stood on Casey's left and Mikey on her right. Casey's solo debut was being promoted and marketed as one of the biggest movies to hit the industry in years. It was rumored that Casey's movie could even put Jenna Jamison out of business.

***

Since their arrival in Los Angeles, Dominique and Casey had had vastly different experiences with the industry. An L.A. film company, Hot Licks Productions, had taken one look at Dominique and said they would "stick her in" when they could. Dominique had been called to do a few scenes when they wanted Casey to get licked or when they wanted to get the male actors hard enough to carry out short takes with Casey. Dominique felt degraded and disheartened.

One filming producer, Sylvester Sin, had been very blunt with Jordan. "We just don't have any use for the black girl anymore." Jordan had argued that the two were a "package deal," but Sylvester had threatened to let them both go if he couldn't just use Casey. The producer offered Jordan a solution to his dilemma. "There is a black film company called Sunshine Productions. They take her type," Sylvester said, handing Jordan a card. Afraid of losing his only source of income, Jordan agreed to take Dominique to the black film company.

"What the fuck is this, Jordan?" Dominique asked, looking out the car window at the decrepit looking house located in a rough suburb of L.A.

"Yo, this is the address they gave me for Sunshine Productions," Jordan said, ducking his head to examine the building.

"This shit gets worse and worse. Casey gets bonbons and fucking caviar sets and I get a crackhouse?" Dominique screamed, lighting up a cigarette.

"Diamond, the industry is different for black girls than it is for white girls. Casey went mainstream . . . I don't know what to tell you. You can either stop complaining or get the fuck out and be broke," he said harshly.

Dominique and Jordan got out of the car and walked up to the address. Dominique felt tears burning behind her eyes.

She couldn't believe the disparity in treatment between her and Casey. Dominique had learned the hard way that black girls very rarely become major porn stars in mainstream, big-budget porn movies. When their movies first starting blowing up, as hard as she had worked, Dominique had been seen as just an incidental to Casey's performances.

Jordan pressed a small rectangular bell at the left of the battered door. A scary, looking giant of a man yanked open the door. "Yeah," the man grunted.

"Mikey Cuntmore and Sylvester Sin sent me," Jordan announced.

The giant motioned Jordan and Dominique through the door. The high scent of several different perfumes hit Dominique's nose and she scrunched her face in response.

"Dayum," Jordan echoed, covering his nose with his fore-arm. Dominique didn't have a good feeling about this, but she was plain broke. The last time she had gotten paid, it was a fraction of the percentage Casey received. Dominique saw this as her chance to make her own money—enough to get her back to New York, at least.

"I'm Mr. Wonderful," a tall, skinny, dark-skinned man with a ponytail introduced himself as Jordan and Dominique sat in the kitchen of the house. The house had been converted into a low-budget studio. There were no cranes and movie lights; instead, tripods and cheap photography umbrella lights on stands littered the rooms inside.

"I'm Jordan Bleu and this is Diamond Tiara," Jordan introduced, extending his hand for a shake. Dominique puffed on her second cigarette.

"I've heard you are the manager for Denver Peaks. Man, that's some good shit," Mr. Wonderful complimented, his eyes lighting up.

Dominique rolled her eyes. "Here we go again. Are we here to discuss her or are we here to talk about me?" she asked.

"A feisty one, aren't you?" Mr. Wonderful said, grabbing a handful of his crotch, eyeing her seductively. "I don't know what you're used to, but I pay two-fifty a movie," he said, getting right to the point. Dominique turned her head and looked at Jordan with raised eyebrows.

"Everybody here works. Ain't no fake-ass short takes that get edited together for one big movie, either. I like to give my viewers the real thing, not the same scene over and over again," Mr. Wonderful explained. Jordan was shaking his head up and down in agreement. "So in other words, you either agree to fuck or no deal," Mr. Wonderful said.

"It's all good. She's down," Jordan agreed on her behalf.

"Ain't this some shit," Dominique spat. Jordan sealed the deal on a handshake. There were no contracts; no waivers; no high-priced medical physicals. Just fuck 'em and get paid.

A week after their first meeting with Sunshine Productions, Dominique sat on the bootleg set and took a long drag on the blunt Mr. Wonderful had given her. It seemed to enhance what already flowed in her system.

"You ready?" he asked, noticing her low eyes.

"I was obviously born ready," Dominique answered non-committally.

"Well, then, it's show time, baby," he said, reaching down into her blouse and pinching one of her nipples.

Dominique walked over to the queen-sized bed that sat in the middle of the room. On the left side of the bed was one small wooden nightstand with a huge bottle of baby oil sitting on it, and several condoms. Dominique jumped up on the bed like she was happy to be there, the drugs making it easier. Mr. Wonderful called in his three best male stars: Sizzla; Aries; and Long Dong Shiver. They looked at Dominique like she was a plate of their favorite food.

"First, you and Sizzla going to do a one-on-one, and Long Dong is gonna come in and join," Mr. Wonderful directed.

Dominique flipped over onto her stomach and inched to the edge of the bed. Sizzla stood at the edge, his dick in hand, waiting. Dominique moved her face closer to his obviously pumped-up flesh and she could smell the cheap Irish Spring soap still on it. Closing her eyes, she licked her lips, and took him into her mouth.

"Yeah, just like that, Diamond girl. You know how to do it," Mr. Wonderful called out like a coach. Dominique moved her mouth up and down on Sizzla's dark flesh, the vein pulsing on her tongue. As she continued, she felt the bed moving. Long Dong Shiver had climbed on the bed behind her. His rippled muscles and hard body had Dominique a bit concerned. She stopped her act to see what was going on.

"Don't stop, Diamond. He won't bite," Mr. Wonderful instructed. Long Dong pulled Dominique up onto her knees as she went back to her original act of fellatio. She felt him pouring the cheap baby oil onto her ass and he used his hands to mix it in, swiping up and down her crack. Then he took his unbelievably large manhood and drove it into her.

"Oww!" Dominique yelped, sharp pains surging through her abdomen as he plowed her from the back. Sizzla grabbed her hair and pulled her face back into his crotch forcefully. She was being banged from both ends. Dominique gagged as Sizzla didn't take any mercy on her mouth. Saliva involuntarily dripped from her lips and mixed with the tears that were coming from her eyes. She could hear Mr. Wonderful's voice, but her ears had begun to ring so loudly that she could no longer hear his instructions.

Long Dong slapped Dominique's skin unmercifully. The more excited he got, the harder he hit her ass cheeks, causing them to sting. Finally, Sizzla removed himself from her mouth.

He grabbed her hair and pulled her face up toward the camera. Dominique felt like her neck would break from the awkward position.

"Aggh," Sizzla growled, spewing a thick wad of his semen all over her face.

Mr. Wonderful ran over with the camera and panned in as Sizzla swiped it all over her.

"That's the money shot!" Mr. Wonderful called out.

When they were done with her, Dominique gathered her things to head toward the little makeshift dressing/bedroom they had for the girls. Before she could make it out of the room, Mr. Wonderful walked over and handed her $250 and two vials of crack. They exchanged a knowing glance before she raced into the bathroom. With the shower turned on full blast, she sat in the tub with her knees drawn into her chest and sobbed until she lost her breath.

When Dominique was done scalding her skin off in the bathroom, she came out to the kitchen. Mr. Wonderful's powerful voice, echoed by moans and grunts, filtered through the house. Mr. Wonderful had begun filming other short movies that would be added to Dominique's DVD. On her way to the refrigerator, she noticed a girl sitting at the kitchen table smoking a Black & Mild.

"What's up?" the girl asked. Dominique looked at her like she was crazy. She wasn't in the mood for no jealous female bullshit today.

"I'm Carissa," the girl introduced herself. She wore a long, lace-front, Beyoncé-style wig over a heavily made-up face complete with long, fake eyelashes.

"I'm Diamond," Dominique returned.

"You already finished filming?" Carissa asked.

"Yeah, I'm done. You work here too?" Dominique asked

"Yup, I'm Sunshine's biggest anal star," Carissa boasted like it was something to be proud of.

"Oh," Dominique said, lowering her eyes and taking a seat at the table.

Carissa looked at her long and hard. "Hold up! You the girl who was in those movies with that new white girl everybody talkin' about, right?" Carissa asked.

"Yeah, that's me," Dominique admitted.

"Well, shit! What the hell you doin' in this low-ass budget joint? You already went mainstream," Carissa inquired.

"Those white boys didn't want me. Those muthafuckas are prejudiced as hell," Dominique spewed, eyeing Carissa's neatly twisted joint.

"I know what you mean," Carissa agreed, passing Dominique the joint like it was a peace pipe. Dominique gladly accepted. She took a long drag and inhaled. They puff-puff-passed until the joint was smoked down to a roach.

"Where you from, Diamond?" Carissa asked.

"New York . . . and don't ask what the fuck I'm doing way out in L.A. fucking for less than the amount of money I could make on the street," Dominique said.

"Well, why are you here?" Carissa asked.

"I guess you can say I was loyal to some people who didn't have the same values as me. I'm trying to get back to New York, though," Dominique explained.

"I always wanted to go to the Big Apple. I'm from Compton," Carissa said wistfully.

"I will keep that in mind when I'm ready to bounce. I probably could use the company," Dominique said, smiling.

Dominique and Carissa talked for hours. It was the most fun Dominique had had since her relationship with Casey had become strained. Friends were in short order, but to Dominique, Carissa seemed a pretty solid type.

***

Dominique left the press conference for Casey's solo debut with a lot on her mind. She took a cab back to their rented condo so that she could smoke her bones in peace. Dominique knew that Jordan and Casey wouldn't be home anytime soon since they were headed to the party Mikey was throwing for Casey. They were also supposed to be meeting with representatives from *Playboy* to negotiate her first photo shoot for the magazine's new calendar.

When Dominique made it to the condo, she was happy to be alone. She walked around inside like it belonged all to her. She tried on Casey's new wardrobe. So many sexy lingerie costume designers had been sending Casey their new designs so that they could get free advertising in her movies.

Dominique looked through the closets and drawers and accidentally came across a small safe hidden behind a monumental stack of sneakers. Curious to see if she could crack the combination, she twisted and twisted, left right left . . . right left right. Dominique thought about numbers that would be significant to Jordan. Since she had met him, she knew that although he hated his mother, he sent her flowers and a card every year on July 31. He'd also told her that his mother was born in 1959. Dominique twisted the safe combo knob left seven, right thirty-one, left fifty-nine. "Fuckin' bingo!" she whispered when the lock clicked open.

Dominique was spooked when she first observed the contents of the safe. There were several rubber-banded stacks of one hundred–dollar bills; plastic baggies full of different colored pills; and two handguns. Dominique's first instinct was to take the money and run, but self doubt and fear caused her to hurriedly close the safe and exit the closet before her roommates returned.

***

Casey's solo movie, *Denver's Peaks* was a smashing success. Casey and Jordan were making unheard-of money for being newcomers to the industry. Casey's face was on every porn magazine. Those sky blue eyes and that golden hair had propelled her to the top. Casey was so busy lavishing in the fame that she barely missed Dominique's company. Jordan was doing much of the same. He'd recently purchased a new luxury car and several new watches and pieces of jewelry. He and Casey were on the L.A. party scene almost every night.

One night, the two were partying at Skybar with tall types of celebrities including several rappers and some of the players from the L.A. Lakers who were huge Denver Peaks fans. Casey was the center of attention and looked like a goddess. She wore an all-white mini-dress so short that if she had shifted wrong everyone would be able to see up into her womb. Her hair was twisted up into a messy but stylish bun, and she rocked the hottest sparkly Christian Louboutins that hadn't even been released yet. Casey was popping her pills and chasing them down with expensive Ace of Spades champagne. She giggled incessantly, high as a kite and feeling larger than life. Anna Nicole had nothing on her.

Jordan complemented her in his usual all-black linen, his new jewels and watch, upgrading his style from hood rich to almost wealthy. Relishing in his newfound fame, he didn't notice Dominique making her way toward them until it was too late. Jordan squinted to make sure his eyes weren't deceiving him.

"Fuck," he whispered under his breath, noticing that Dominique looked completely tossed. "I'll be right back," he whispered in Casey's ear, never alerting her to what was going on. Casey smiled and giggled with a music producer who apparently was a big fan.

Dominique forged ahead, pushing people out of her way.

Her hair weave was a tangled mess, her cheap spandex dress was baggy on her skinny frame and her face was ashen with too much misapplied make-up. They met in the middle of the crowded club, toe to toe.

"Where do you think you goin' lookin' like this?" Jordan asked harshly, grabbing her arm.

"I'm coming to congratulate Casey on her number-one hit movie. Ain't this her party?" Dominique slurred, clearly under the influence of some drug.

"You should've gone home and got dressed first," Jordan said, pushing her back toward the door.

"Well, if somebody would've fuckin' told me there was a party in honor of my protégé I woulda been here front and center," Dominique spat indignantly, backing up as Jordan pushed forward.

"Look, Diamond, obviously you had too much of whatever it is you fuckin' with these days. Don't make me go up top on ya ass in here. Go home and sleep it off." Jordan gritted his teeth, propelling her through the crowd.

"Go home! Go the fuck home? You just dismissing me like that? I don't fuckin' deserve to enjoy the fame and fortune? I made both of you, muthafuckas! You and that fuckin' farm bitch of yours got rich off my back and don't you forget it!" Dominique screamed, causing some of the partygoers to turn in their direction.

Jordan looked around, the heat of embarrassment climbing up his neck and rising to his face. He had an image to maintain. He didn't want anyone to see him throttle her ass, but his patience was running low. Jordan grabbed Dominique by the neck and lifted her off of her feet. The crowd cleared a path and watched the exchange take place. She kicked and thrashed against him, clawing at his hands as he cut off her airway.

"What's going on?" one of the club's bouncers asked.

"I got this," Jordan assured him as he forcefully tossed Dominique out the door. She screamed as she fell to the ground, breaking three fake nails and scraping her elbow and the left side of her face.

"Jordan, you gon' treat me like this after all I did for you, muthafucka?" Dominique cried out, pulling herself up off the ground. "You ain't gon' never have no fuckin' luck, you bastard!" Dominique cursed as she limped away.

Dominique went to Carissa's house where she stayed whenever she wasn't at Sunshine Productions performing some lewd act for money. When Carissa pulled back the door, she put her hand over her mouth. "What the hell happened to you?" she asked.

"That bastard . . . That bastard!" Dominique screamed over and over again, falling to her knees.

"You need something?" Carissa asked. Dominique's face lit up. She scrambled up off the floor and turned over her pocketbook until her stem fell out. Carissa handed her the goods and Dominique prepped her pipe. With her hands shaking, she let the poison ease her pain. Carissa was there for her. That's all that mattered.

Dominique stayed with Carissa for the next two weeks. Between their degrading stints at Sunshine, they got high together. They would have their little bit of movie pay spent and owed out to the dope man before they even got it in their hands.

Mr. Wonderful had taken notice that Dominique didn't look as pretty as she did when she first arrived. He wasn't about to keep filming a crackhead. Although Carissa smoked, she also ate, so her body was not gaunt and drawn up.

Mr. Wonderful finally fired Dominique. She had gotten the news the same day she'd heard that Casey had been nominated for an AVN award, which was like the Oscars of the porn industry.

***

Casey looked at all of the designer dresses that had been sent to her for her appearance at the awards show. Designers treated the event just as importantly as the Hollywood-style awards shows, hoping that the biggest porn stars chose their outfits to wear for the night. Casey had never really been into fashion. She usually let Dominique pick out her outfits. Lately, it had been Jordan who dressed her. She slumped down on the bed and put her fist up to her cheek. Where was Diamond when she needed her?

Jordan had told Casey that Dominique was away filming, but Casey hadn't seen her in weeks. Whenever she wasn't too blitzed to walk after a party or some appearance, Casey would check Dominique's bedroom for her and it was always empty. Casey decided to call Dominique's cell phone to invite her friend to the AVNs just in case she won. Casey dialed Dominique's number but it was disconnected. Casey didn't understand how this came to be, since Jordan paid for their phone service. She threw her cell phone on the bed and promised that she would make Jordan find Diamond for this special event. It would be Casey's first time in Las Vegas and she couldn't go without Diamond.

"Casey! You ready to go?" Jordan called out. Casey came out of the bedroom half dressed, giggling and walking seductively.

"What the fuck you doin'?" Jordan barked, looking her up and down.

"I'm not going until Diamond gets here," Casey slurred, a stupid, lazy grin on her face.

"I told you Diamond is filming, so let's go!" Jordan barked.

"I'm not going without Diamond," Casey insisted, the pills she had swallowed fifteen minutes earlier giving her courage. Jordan's eyes hooded over and he grabbed his bottle of Mylanta and took a swig.

"I'm not fuckin' around . . . Let's go," he growled, the white ring from the medicine on his top lip making him look like an evil version of a "Got Milk?" ad. Casey busted out laughing.

"Or else what?" she teased, lifting an unsteady finger to wipe his lip. Jordan rushed into her with the might of a bulldozer, backing her up against the wall. He grabbed her neck and squeezed, fire flashing in his eyes.

"You will get ready now. You won't fuck this up for me," he huffed like a crazed madman. He released a gagging Casey before he could leave rings on her neck. She held onto her neck and raced into the bedroom, tears streaming down her face.

"Diamond where are you?" Casey croaked in despair.

Dominique walked up and down Sepulveda Boulevard barely able to attract a five-dollar trick. She sauntered like she still had that umph to make a cool G in one night. Dominique hadn't really taken a good look at herself lately. She had aged ten years in her face and the few clothes she had hung off her skinny frame like oversized rags. She dipped and dodged, careful to make sure none of the ruthless Boulevard pimps spotted her infringing on their tracks. Dominique refused to get involved with another pimp. Every day she told herself she was just trying to get up enough money to make it back to New York. Dominique had decided that L.A. wasn't for her and she had already paid a steep price for her fifteen minutes of fame. She hadn't saved up her plane fare yet, but she usually made just enough to cop her drugs.

A car finally pulled up. Flashing an ashy-lip smile, she jumped in. "Whatchu want, fuck or suck?" she said dryly. The old white man signed and pointed to his crotch. "Ain't this about a bitch. This muthafucka is deaf!" Dominique growled, lowering her head into his lap.

***

After a few hours out on the track, exhausted and damn near broke, Dominique went back to Carissa's house where she had been holed up for weeks. When she got inside, Carissa was sitting on the couch smoking her crack-laced blunt. That was the difference between them—Carissa liked the upper and downer effect of the weed and rock cocaine mixture, and Dominique got hers right from the pipe. These days she left the expensive-ass heroin alone.

"What's up, girl?" Carissa asked. "You look like shit," she commented.

"Well, I'm not in a bed fuckin' for the cameras no more," Dominique grumbled, referring to the fact that Carissa was still allowed to work at Sunshine Productions even though she had a habit too.

"Hey, I saw that your friends are going to be at the AVN awards in Vegas," Carissa told her.

"I could give a fuck less," Dominique spat, rolling her eyes and frantically fishing around in her purse for her stem. She needed to get her mind right.

"I hear you, but maybe now you can go get the rest of your shit since crazy man ain't gonna be there," Carissa reminded her. Dominique had bragged about her fur coat, diamond bracelets and hundreds of shoes. Judging from the way Dominique looked, Carissa just thought Dominique was delusional over the little bit of fame she got while working with Casey.

Carissa's words took a minute to process. Through the haze of the smoke cloud that surrounded her face, a light bulb went off in Dominique's head. She still had a key to the condo. Unless Jordan had changed the locks, she could get in and out with her stuff in no time. Dominique blew out her last bit of smoke, her heart racing and palms sweaty with anticipation. "Come with me and I'll make it worth your while," Dominique said as she reached for her purse.

When Dominique fit the key into the condo's front door and heard it click, her heart skipped a beat. She raced inside like a cat burglar with Carissa on her heels.

"Go in that room and get some of those clothes and shoes out the closet," Dominique instructed, her hands trembling like a real fiend. When Carissa was out of sight, Dominique ducked into Jordan's closet. She prayed silently that the safe was still there. She maneuvered her skinny body around all of the new designer threads Jordan and Casey had collected in her absence.

"Fuckin' traitors," she mumbled. She twisted the combo wheel like a careful jewel thief, and when the safe popped open, so did her eyes. Dominique felt a little trickle of urine wet her underwear in her excitement. "Bingo, hot damn," she sang to herself.

She contemplated leaving a few dollars and some jewelry behind, but memories of how dirty Jordan had done her left Dominique without a conscience.

"Muthafucka, you shoulda changed the locks," Dominique giggled as she stuffed the rubber-banded stacks of money, both guns, a box of ammunition, a diamond bracelet, a Breitling and a stack of Treasury bills into a tote bag stolen from Casey's closet.

Smiling from ear to ear, Dominique called out to Carissa who was still raiding Dominique's clothing and accessories.

"C'mon, girl, let's go," Dominique said. Carissa had the chinchilla draped over her back as she dragged a bag full of newfound treasures.

Chapter Thirteen

Revenge

Brice sat outside of Jordan's mother's house in Harlem every day after he received the information from Casey. He had watched the door like a crazed stalker, not really sure what he would do if he saw Jordan with his sister. Jordan had never shown up, and when Brice finally knocked on the door and encountered Trina King, he realized why her son was probably so fucked up.

Today, Brice sat nursing a drink inside of the crowded Sugar Hill restaurant/club on Dekalb Avenue waiting for the dude to show up. Brice had all of the information he needed on Jordan Bleu, thanks to Casey and Dominique. He had looked at his sister's naked test shots over and over again. The thought of her being touched by a man made him grind his teeth almost to crumbs. Brice studied the addresses where Ciara might be holed up. He had mapped out a few routes in and out—side streets, determined whether there was high traffic, what the night life was like. He played out in his mind the scenarios of when he met Jordan face to face. Brice knew he only had one shot at this and he planned on walking away with his sister healthy and alive. During their meeting, each time Casey and Dominique told him another story about Jordan, Brice saw himself adding one more bullet to Jordan's dome.

Brice wanted this plate of revenge to be served ice fucking cold, just he and Jordan's punk-bitch ass. No cops, no gangstas, nothing but the two of them like cowboys at high noon. Brice tried to be patient searching for his sister, but the legal way wasn't fast enough. He could've given the information to the crackpot missing persons detectives but he knew they would just tarnish his sister's reputation even further and make them think she was some kind of street slut runaway. In his assessment, justice didn't exist for his people—not even for a cop's sister. Brice immediately took to the streets to find some of his old cohorts so he could get his hands on a gun and bulletproof vest, since he'd had his taken away when he was suspended. Brice had officially said "fuck the police!" Doing shit the right way wouldn't save his sister from an uncertain future.

Casey had told Brice that Jordan was probably still right there in New York, hiding out with Ciara. She told him that Jordan's primary method of making money was putting young girls on the streets. His other avenue of income was the porn industry. Brice cringed thinking about his sister involved in either activity. He would fucking kill Jordan with his own hands when he found him. What difference did it make now? His reputation had already been tarnished in the department.

Brice hadn't gotten much sleep, nor had he eaten a decent meal in the last few days. He had lost everything that meant something to him. He couldn't help but feel like he deserved it for what he had done to Earl. In the end, it had been a hefty price to pay to protect his dirty past. Listening to Casey and Dominique speak about their struggles had done something to him inside. He realized how much he had taken away from his rape victim's life. Brice could picture her contorted face, smell the boys' body fluids on her, feel the resistance of her body saying no. He threw his head back and took a swig of his Hennessy.

"B-Boy, my nig, is that you?" Brice heard the familiar voice from behind and felt a pat on his shoulder. He turned around slowly.

"Pop! My old dude. What's good man?" Brice said, exchanging a hand slap and shoulder bump with the man. Pop was one of the street dudes Brice and Earl had grown up with. While Pop and Brice were not as close as he and Earl, Pop was around enough when they were younger to get into several mischievous capers with them. Unlike Earl, Pop was always a smooth dude. Even as a kid, he did his dirt on the low-making all the parents in the neighborhood refer to him as the "good one." Pop wasn't into the fifteen-minutes-of-fame thing. He didn't commit blatant and brash crimes like Earl did. Pop was more of a behind-the-scenes type of dude. Pop had made his living on the streets but had turned his dirty money into legitimate investments. Pop also didn't know until Earl's funeral that his old friend B-Boy was a cop. Although he knew the story surrounding Earl's death, it had been spun that Earl had tried to mirk Brice. Pop knew that Earl could be a wild boy, but even though he was skeptical of all cops, he didn't hold Brice responsible for Earl's death. Pop figured one day he'd have to call in a favor. It just so happened that right now, the tables were turned.

"I'm chillin', man. I saw the news. That shit is crazy," Pop said, offering his sympathy.

"I got some information. I might know where she is holed up," Brice told him, leaning in so no one else could hear over the blaring music.

"A'ight, so whatchu need, my dude?" Pop asked. Brice laid it out for him. He needed some heavy artillery and some body armor. Brice wasn't trying to use his own personal off-duty weapon for this job.

"You need some back up?" Pop asked. "Because from the sound of it, you planning to go Rambo on a niggah," Pop commented.

"Nah, this is my fight. I'm not hiding behind a gun and shield. I'm taking it back to the streets. This muthafucka is as good as dead," Brice said, holding his glass so tight his knuckles paled.

"I feel you, my nig. Real talk, I hope all goes well with your sister and shit. Meet me tomorrow down Broadway and Halsey. I gotchu," Pop assured him. Brice was grateful that he could rely on his old friend for help.

"Yo, let me get a round of Hen . . . one for me and one for my manz," Brice told the bartender. Pop pulled up a seat next to Brice. They had a bit of catching up to do.

Brice had turned his back on the one place that had his back—the streets. But right now, that was the only thing he could rely upon. The NYPD certainly was not looking out for his best interests.

Alton watched as the little girl undressed, her little flower-bud breasts making him sweat. He closed his eyes and prayed over and over again. "Our father, who art in heaven. . . ." He had to ask God's forgiveness for his sins. Things had gone over the top. The sensations and urges just wouldn't go away. The thoughts had kept him up all night. They had made him angry and ashamed. As always, Alton took it out on his wife. He didn't know how to tell her that he had a sickness. He had never told anyone how he had molested his own sister as a child and that his overly religious parents had hidden it and made the subject taboo in their home.

Alton had decided to just try it with a girl, since adult women didn't satisfy his insatiable urges. He told himself, *Just this once.* He was really afraid because at church on Sundays he was surrounded by them. Hundreds of beautiful little teenage girls that he constantly fantasized about. Alton was afraid if he didn't get it out of his system, he'd have the urge to touch one of them again.

He had found this guy online. When he met up with him to pay him for the girl, Alton immediately became spooked because the man's face was battered and bandaged. The man took the money and turned over the girl. Alton brought her into the cellar of the church through the back. He could not take a chance with going to any hotel. He was too famous for that. The little girl barely spoke English, so it was more hand motions than verbal communication. Alton wanted to play his new movies while he did the act. He clicked on the computer as the girl touched his body. When he put on Denver's old movie, he was immediately turned on . . . until his wife's face came on the screen.

Alton had told Dominique that he would be doing his sick and shut-in visits all day. She decided that it would be a good time to go to the church office where he kept all of their financial paperwork. Dominique wanted to leave. After the last beating, she had decided that, like Mama Grady said, "evil is evil," and Dominique had had enough. Although to her knowledge there was no one at the church, she was so conditioned to sneak and be wary of Alton, that she crept like a mouse through the church's hallways. Dominique had lifted Alton's spare keys. Just as she passed the door to his office, she heard the moaning. Startled, Dominique stopped dead in her tracks. She was so afraid, she temporarily lost her breath. When she finally recognized Alton's voice, she almost fainted, but was unable to move.

Dominique swallowed hard, and her legs felt like someone had weighed them down with lead. She was finally able to compose herself. She crept toward the sounds. Dominique blinked rapidly as she peered through the small crack in the door. She threw her hand up to her mouth to muffle her labored breathing. Tears immediately burst from the corners of her eyes. She had to get out of there before she did something she would regret.

Dominique stumbled back up the steps and outside to her car. Feeling like she would hurl, she slid into the driver's seat. Betrayed again, she rocked back and forth and slammed her fist against the steering wheel. Dominique had really finally had enough. What she had seen was enough to send the sanest person into a psychiatric ward. She thought about going home, digging up the carpet and coming back with her gun, but that would be too easy for evil husband.

"Another no-good man," she whispered out loud. She refused to let another tear drop. Dominique was tired of being sick and tired. She was tired of being abused. She would wait, plan then execute.

Dominique pulled her car off the street and began driving toward her home. Her cell phone rang . . . It was Casey.

"Hello," she answered, barely able to speak with so much running through her mind.

"Diamond, I want you to do the interview with me," Casey blurted out.

"I can't," Dominique told her. She had finally agreed to help the detective and that was enough.

"I want people to know your story. I want them to know how strong you are and I need you there," Casey cried.

"I don't think you understand. You didn't go through what I went through. You didn't have to rebuild your life from absolutely nothing. And call me Dominique!" she screamed and cried at the same time, disconnecting the line.

Dominique pulled her car over to the side of the road and closed her eyes. She knew the reason she was hesitant was because she had immediately been thinking about her husband. She had conditioned herself to take care of everyone else but herself. Maybe Casey was right. Maybe this was what Dominique needed and deserved—a chance to tell her story to the world. A chance to heal all of the emotional wounds she had buried. Another shot at fame, but at a price that was on her terms—terms she could afford.

Jordan answered his phone in a huff. He had been so busy getting his movies done that he rarely ever left Mikey's studio. "Wait . . . calm the fuck down!" Jordan barked into the receiver. "The sister of a cop? What the fuck are you talkin' about, D'Guilio?" Jordan asked the man on the other end. His stomach began roiling and his palms got sweaty. "Media coverage?" he grumbled as he looked over at the girl. She lay in a fetal position too high to move without prompting. Jordan had brought out the heavy duty shit to keep her in line—Rohypnol, a.k.a. roofies, the date-rape drug. She was easier to manage that way. Jordan looked over at her, a feeling of disgust washing over him. A brother who was a cop, who was also actively searching for her, was definitely not part of the plan. Jordan sucked in his bottom lip. She was no longer an investment, she was a definite problem. Jordan cracked open a fresh bottle of Mylanta and downed the entire thing in one swallow. He had to make a move . . . and fast.

Brice ran his fingers over the cold steel of the shiny silver .45-caliber Desert Eagle special. Pop had come through big time. The fact that he knew how to shoot it properly made him feel not just powerful, but invincible. Brice was well aware that in the streets, shooters always cocked their guns to the side like they were playing cowboys and Indians, which almost always assured a missed shot. Being trained up, Brice knew how to use his sights to hit the center mass; after all, he was a five-ring expert marksman.

"You get me inside and then you get the fuck outta dodge, you hear me?" Brice whispered to Casey. She shook her head up and down. She really wanted to see Jordan suffer, but she knew this was risky at best.

"It's me, Dave . . . Casey," she said into the intercom system. Brice stood off to the side. His police training told him that he was being stupid. He walked into possible danger like a fool with no kind of backup . . . a one-man army. It was too late to back down; too much was at stake.

When Dave pulled back the doors, Casey smiled and stepped aside. Brice rounded the corner and pounced on the man so fast, Dave let out several farts in rapid succession.

"Where the fuck is he?" Brice growled, his hot breath blowing on Dave's face.

"Who ya lookin' for?" Dave croaked out.

"Jordan, muthafucka, you know who!" Brice said in a low harsh whisper. He didn't want to give anyone else in the suite a chance to come out with weapons blazing.

"Ask Mikey . . . I don't know," Dave said. Brice released him with a shove and stepped over his body. He stormed down a long hallway toward the sounds at the back of the suite. Brice used his raid boots to kick the door open. He was startled by a high-pitched scream from a woman. He spotted a fat white man hovering over a bed with a camera. The man's eyes were stretched so wide he looked almost like a cartoon.

"Where the fuck is that coward Jordan Bleu?" Brice yelled out, rushing toward the director.

"He left, man. I swear . . . he ain't here. Said something about leaving town. He called the cop guy who gets the girls for him. I don't know, man. . . ." Mikey stuttered. He had already dropped the camera and put his hands up in front of him as if they could shield him from the big-ass gun Brice aimed at his fat tits.

"What? A cop?" Brice asked.

"Yeah, man. Jordan got girls on the street and he gets girls for underground movies from this white guy . . . a cop," Mikey blabbed, his words rolling off his tongue so fast he couldn't even get them out right.

"Where does he go?" Brice asked.

"Man, I don't know, I swear," Mikey pleaded. Brice walked over to him and hit him on the back of the neck with the butt of the gun. Mikey screamed out. "Now, where does he go to get the girls?" Brice asked calmly.

"All I got is the cell phone number . . . I swear, man . . . that's all I got," Mikey moaned, his fat girth spilled over the floor like a beached whale. He directed Brice to his desk. There was a piece of paper there with a number and no name. "Jordan had written that down and forgot it there—that's the new number the man gave him," Mikey explained.

Brice folded the paper into his pocket. He looked at the three girls sitting naked, cowering in a corner. "How old are these fuckin' girls?" Brice asked, coming back to stand over Mikey with the gun aimed at Mikey's head.

"They told me they were eighteen," Mikey whined, sounding like a straight bitch.

"Everybody get dressed and get out of here!" Brice yelled to the girls. Their faces were filled with horror. They scrambled around like hens running from the slaughter house.

"If you contact Jordan and tell him I was here, I will kill you myself," Brice threatened Mikey before he took off.

Brice's hands trembled as he dialed Detective Page's number. He exhaled when Page picked up. "I need you to do a reverse look-up on a number," Brice said, his voice shaky. Detective Page agreed and told Brice he would call him back. When the phone rang, Brice fumbled with it, his nerves on edge. The number returned no information on the public Internet. Brice was going to have to call in a favor to the Feds. "Fuck!" he screamed after hanging up with the Detective.

Brice called an F.B.I. agent he had met while standing patrol on a dignitary homicide. Special Agent Lisa Striker was a hot-ass black female agent who had taken a liking to Brice. Brice thought she was so damn beautiful—she reminded him of Nia Long, who he'd been in love with since *Boyz n the Hood*.

After a few dates, Brice and Lisa learned that two type-A law enforcement personalities weren't so good together, as they were always competing. Agent Striker had called recently when she'd heard about his sister. She had told Brice she would've loved to get in on the search for Ciara, but the Bureau had prevented Striker from getting involved since the NYPD had classified the case as a runaway.

When Agent Striker picked up the line, Brice gave her the number. She told him she would go into the Bureau's databases and get right back to him. She called back within minutes.

"I hope you're sitting down," she told Brice. "The name is listed as unknown . . . but the billing address came up. When I ran the billing address, it came back to Anthony and Carmelita D'Guilio. When I ran Anthony D'Guilio to match the address, he came up as a NYPD detective!" Agent Striker announced.

Brice thought his heart would thunder out of his chest. "Muthafucka! Muthafucka!" Brice screamed so loud his throat itched.

"Brice . . . what is it?" she asked, shocked by his outburst.

"I want you to meet me. I may have stumbled onto a human trafficking ring that has my sister," Brice announced. Renegade suspended cop or not, he knew this was going to be an all-out operation.

D'Guilio rushed out of the precinct when he received the call. His blood was boiling inside. "How stupid could he be?" D'Guilio mumbled. He was so caught up in thought that he didn't notice the new tail on his back.

"Why the fuck did you bring her here?" D'Guilio barked, spit spewing from his face.

"I need to get rid of her and get the fuck out of here," Jordan said, moving around like he was being bitten by little bugs.

"Not here! Not with all these girls right in the next room!" D'Guilio screamed. "The Russians will have my fuckin' head on a platter," he said, pounding his right fist into his left hand.

"This is the only place I could go. I need to leave her here where she can be guarded until I can figure something out," Jordan said weakly, pacing now.

"What you need to do is let her go home and you get the fuck outta dodge. Never to mention my name, never to mention this place, never to fuckin' bring your black ass back again," D'Guilio said, pointing in Jordan's face. "You ain't man enough to put a fuckin' end to this because she is a cop's fuckin' sister? You would risk losing everything?" D'Guilio asked, lifting his personal weapon from his shoulder rig. Jordan's world started closing in on him. He was taken back to the apartment with C-Lo and the girl. He started seeing visions of the little dead girl from the East New York apartment.

"You need to do what you gotta do. They think she is a runaway anyway," D'Guilio said. "I'd rather sacrifice one girl than have the fuckin' Russian mafia come after me and my entire family because I fucked with a dickhead like you," he spat. He stormed over to where Ciara sat huddled and crying in a corner.

"Please, I just want to go home," she begged.

"Your brother is a fuckin' troublemaker. He is such a hero, but he couldn't save you," D'Guilio raised his weapon over her.

"No! Pa-leese!" she screamed, throwing her hands up in defense. Three shots rang into the air, followed by silence.

Brice's feet had been moving at the speed of light when the shots were fired. His hands shook uncontrollably and sweat dripped from every pore in his body. Detective D'Guilio's body lurched forward, falling just inches from Ciara.

Ciara cried out, covering her face with her hands.

"Be careful, the other one has a gun too!" Special Agent Striker screamed, her gun still smoking at the tip.

"Stay there, Ciara! Drop your fuckin' weapon!" Brice screamed as Jordan leveled his weapon at him. They both pointed at each other, looking like two cowboys at a showdown.

"I'm not going out like this, son. Not over no bitch," Jordan said, holding his position. Brice could hear his own breath in his ears.

"We just both gonna have to die," Jordan kept talking shit, but was visibly shaking like a frostbite victim.

"Well, prepare to die, cowboy," Brice stated calmly.

"Fuck you!" Jordan screamed out, cocking his gun to the side. Brice seized his moment and shot Jordan in the shoulder of his shooting hand. Jordan fell backward, gun flying from his hand.

Brice didn't want him dead. Not yet anyway. Before Brice could reach him, he heard the thunder of feet. When Brice turned around there were a swarm of law enforcement, some NYPD and some F.B.I. Agent Striker had Ciara and was trying to console her.

"Simp . . . you all right?" Detective Page asked, racing over to Brice while the backup stormed Jordan like he had a bomb strapped to him.

"I'm fine," Brice said, dropping his illegal gun on the floor. He knew it would disappear. He ran over to his sister and they hugged so tightly he thought she would stop breathing.

"I'm sorry I failed you," Brice cried into her hair.

"We got an ambulance waiting for her," Detective Page said.

"I guess you back in the spotlight, Simp," Detective Page said, patting Brice on the back.

"Nah. You can keep the lousy fifteen minutes of fame . . . the fuckin' price is too high," Brice replied, holding on to his sister and promising to never let her go.

"The porn industry is a one hundred billion dollar-a year business. A salacious and secretive world that attracts millions of men and women each day. In a world where sex sells, we often wonder about the stars of these oftentimes debasing movies. Tonight on 50 Minutes we turn the tables on a industry that oftentimes portrays itself as a glamorous world where women love to be the object of men, as we sit down with two former self-proclaimed porn queens from two very different walks of life, but who ended up on the same dark path. Join us tonight as we get firsthand stories of women who bargained their bodies for fame and fortune on this segment, "Memoirs of a Porn Queen."

The introduction itself made Dominique's skin crawl. She wanted to back out of the interview, but she had already made it this far. Casey wrung her hands together in her lap as the show's producers strung small microphones to the back of her pants and on her jacket lapel. Casey took her seat next to Dominique on a soft black leather sofa. Diane Saltzer would be sitting in an armless, paisley chair across from them.

They were both prepped with makeup as they watched Ms. Saltzer stroll onto the set and take her seat. Casey thought she looked much younger in person. The director's cue clicked and Casey watched the red digital lights on the wooden structure count down. They were on.

"Two girls, two different races, same industry, nearly the same outcome," Diane Saltzer said to them. Dominique shook her head up and down. Casey had one of her infamous silly grins on her face.

"Dominique, lets start with you," Ms. Saltzer began. "You grew up in Brooklyn, New York, barely educated, and admitted to being on the streets selling your body since you were a teenager," she continued.

"Ahem, yes," Dominique said, her response barely audible.

"How do you make the transition from the streets into the world of pornography?" Ms. Saltzer inquired.

"It's not that hard when you don't know anything else. When you've been selling sex before you ever shopped for your own underwear. When you believe you are not worthy of being loved and when you have never been given any alternatives," Dominique told her.

"Is it easier to be famous for selling sex?" Diane Saltzer asked.

"It's never easy to sell sex. And it's a steep price to pay for fame," Dominique replied.

Diane Saltzer seemed shocked at Dominique's revelations about her childhood, tsking here and there as she relayed some of her more painful memories. Then she turned her attention to Casey.

"How do you go from being the daughter of a Mormon elder to the self-proclaimed Queen of Porn?"

Casey looked at her seriously. The lights that 50 Minutes had set up around her house were hurting her eyes. "I don't think about my past. At the time, that was the life for me. I grew up thinking men were the most important people on the planet and that women should do as they were told. That is what growing up as the daughter of an FLDS elder taught me," Casey answered, shifting in her chair as she wrung her fingers together.

"Well, how does your religion translate into being a world-renowned queen of the sex industry?" Diane Saltzer asked. She wasn't letting Casey off that easily.

"Religion is a hoax. You know what religion did for me? It allowed men to abuse me and use me. Whether you get paid for sex or you're forced into it . . . in my book sex is just sex," Casey said angrily.

"You never think about how much your life has changed? You never think about your family?" Ms. Saltzer pressed as the cameras panned to a picture of Casey's mother, father and four of her siblings.

Casey averted her eyes from the pictures. A golf ball–sized lump was growing in her throat and she willed herself not to cry. "I am human and I think of them often. I could never go back there because of the consequences. I guess that's the price of fame," Casey continued.

"Sex with hundreds of men and even women for money . . . How did that make both of you feel?" Ms. Saltzer asked pointedly, a look of sympathy contorting her face.

"It's what we had to do. Have you ever been homeless with no education and taught to believe sex was your only way of survival?" Dominique posed the rhetorical question.

"But there are programs for girls in situations like yours. How many times did either of you really try to get out of the business?" Ms. Saltzer asked. That question took Dominique's breath away, like someone had just punched her in the diaphragm. It hit Casey equally as hard. She remembered running so hard and fast her feet felt like they were bleeding. She could hear him calling after her. *You ain't shit! You can't leave me, I made you! Where you gonna go? Back to the compound?* An eerie silence pierced the room.

"You both ended up on drugs before leaving the business, correct?" Ms. Saltzer asked.

"That's what the sex business can do to you if you're in it for the wrong reasons," Dominique said, looking for validation from Casey.

"Casey, you were quite famous for a while, but Dominique didn't have the same good fortune, if it could be referred to as such. Why not?" Ms. Saltzer asked, looking from one to the other.

"Just put it this way: the world only sees race differences when they look at us. Racism exists even in the porn business. But no one can take away the fact that although different . . . we grew up exactly the same. The same pain, the same struggles and ultimately we both paid the same price," Dominique answered.

Diane Saltzer seemed to be momentarily speechless. Just like everyone else watching, she probably never considered the human side of the women who sell sex—their emotional pain and struggle.

"Are both of you out of the business?" she asked, trying to break the awkwardness.

Dominique and Casey looked at each other and turned back to her with a solid, "Yes."

"Well, tell us about your experience with leaving the business. How do you just walk away from the money, the attention of millions of men . . . just the fame in general?" Ms. Saltzer asked.

Leaving the business had probably been the hardest part for them both.

Chapter Fourteen

Breaking Free

"*Ain't nobody ever gonna love you. You was tainted from conception because your mother was a whore! You think a man could love you when your daddy ain't give a fuck about you? Who else you got but me? Who else gonna want a throw-away like you?*" Awilda spewed hatred in Dominique's face, brainwashing her into submission once again.

"Mommy," Dominique whispered, delirious and barely able to catch her breath. She could see her mother's face so clearly, it was like she was standing right in front of her.

"Bitch! I ain't ya mama!" Jordan screamed, slamming his huge fist into her face again. She felt the bones in her cheek shatter under her skin and blood spurted from her nose like a turned-over fire hydrant. Dominique felt like someone had hit her in the head with a solid wood baseball bat. Stabs of pain emanated from her nose into her cranium. A scream was stuck somewhere between her diaphragm and her throat. The next hit immediately brought her back to reality, and her mother's face and her aunt's vicious voice faded from her ears.

"I'll teach you," Jordan said in an eerily calm voice as he dragged her across the hot gravel. As soon as Dominique hit the ground, the clouds parted and the sun beamed straight down on her body like a solar spotlight. She was the star of this ass-whooping show. God was trying to tell her something.

Mr. Wonderful had set her up. He had lured her to his studio with a promise to put her in his newest release, but it had all been a ploy concocted by the very man she had heisted three months ago.

"Casey, help me!" Dominique screamed, as Jordan wound his hands deeper into her hair. Casey just stood there with a simple-looking smile on her face. She was too high to help and too afraid of this side of Jordan to risk getting in the middle.

"She can't help you. You wanted to be a porn star, right?" Jordan growled, pulling Dominique's gaunt skeletal frame upright.

"Jordan, please! I will pay you back!" Dominique pleaded. She was well aware of why she was taking this ass whooping.

"You will. Right now!" he huffed, his face in a deep scowl. Casey just stood there in a daze.

"I'm sorry!" Dominique screamed, in a last-ditch effort to save her life. Her screams fell on deaf ears.

As Jordan dragged her on the ground, she felt the skin on her breasts peel back. She felt like somebody poured gasoline all over her body and set her on fire. Her once perfectly erect Chocolate Kiss nipples were being shredded to pieces. The skin on her stomach, thighs and knees were damn near gone, too. Dominique could feel small pebbles sinking into her raw, open flesh, each piece finding a place to embed itself.

Jordan was dragging her around the back of Mr. Wonderful's house, where the dogs were kept.

"Aggh!" She screamed even louder now, thinking Jordan was going to take her back there and kill her. She tried to hold her head up so her face wouldn't drag on the ground, but she couldn't fight against Jordan's strength. Her face had been scraped raw with road rash.

Suddenly the motion stopped. Dominique tried to open her battered eyelids, but the effort wasn't worth the pain. She was so beat up even her eyelids hurt.

"Now tell me where the fuck my money is!" Jordan growled, rolling her over onto her back. Dominique couldn't open her mouth; both of her lips were beating like they had a heart of their own. Blood filled her mouth, covering her teeth like mouthwash. The metallic liquid dripped into the back of her throat. Dominique gurgled, feeling like she was drowning. The pit bulls barked like crazy on their leashes, smelling her blood.

Dominique never thought she would pray for death, but she did now. *God, just take me now. I know the things I've done were horrible, but I never made anyone suffer.*

Jordan's footsteps crunched the gravel next to her ear. Jordan lifted his boot and stomped on her rib cage.

"Jordan, man, I think that's enough," Mr. Wonderful said, coming between Dominique and Jordan.

"Get the fuck back!" Jordan screamed, pulling a gun from his waistband and pointing it at Mr. Wonderful and the other men who stood outside. Casey swallowed hard and covered her eyes. Jordan had changed. He often lost control like this, but lately it had gotten much worse.

"Whoa, whoa man. What type of shit you smokin'?" Mr. Wonderful asked, lifting his hands in surrender. This sure wasn't worth the money Jordan had paid him to turn Dominique over.

"Open the fuckin' dog cages and bring me the breeder," Jordan demanded, his chest heaving.

"Man . . . c'mon. That dog will ravage her," Mr. Wonderful pleaded.

"Not for what I got in mind," Jordan huffed, his gun roving back and forth at the men.

"You are one sick muthafucka!" Mr. Wonderful spat, reluctantly doing as he was told. He gingerly handed Jordan the leash of his biggest dog—a grey, red-nosed, male pit. Jordan smiled wickedly. Holding on to the leash with the dog pulling forward, Jordan walked the dog over to Dominique's writhing body. The dog was going crazy trying to get to her.

"Get up!" Jordan barked, struggling to control the hungry animal. "You wanted to be a porn star, right? Well let's see what you got," Jordan spat. All of the men turned their faces away.

Mr. Wonderful closed his eyes and shook his head. Casey began to cry and shake her head.

"Suck it!" Jordan barked, pulling the dog closer and choking it with the leash to prevent its escape.

"Jordan no, please!" Dominique begged, her face a bloody mess streaked with tears and makeup.

"No? No one says no to me," Jordan hissed. Jordan stepped back, still holding the leash with one hand, and used the other to charge his gun. He placed it to Dominique's temple. Barely able to move her aching body, Dominique was about to do as she was told in a last-ditch effort to save her own life. Jordan snatched the leash, yanking the dog away, just before Dominique could take in a mouthful of the foul, beastly piece of flesh. Instead of going through with his sick acts of torture, Jordan made Dominique think that he was going to let the dog eat her alive. The fear in her eyes made him feel powerful all over again. Jordan let out a loud, cacophonous laugh, as Dominique lay there helpless. He thought of C-Lo and what he had said about when a bitch wasn't useful anymore. Dominique looked up at Casey, barely able to stretch her eyes that far. Why didn't Casey help her when she'd been so good to her all these years?

When Jordan was through with her, he left her there for dead. Casey stepped over her like she was piece of trash. Nobody dared to call the police.

Mr. Wonderful paced back and forth as he looked at Dominique's battered body lying in his backyard. It didn't take him long to realize his culpability if anyone called the authorities. Mr. Wonderful finally decided to help Dominique only to keep his own ass from getting locked up.

As Casey came down off her high, she was racked with guilt. She cried for weeks and was unable to perform successfully on the job. Her name was losing value in the industry. To add to her guilt, Casey recently received news that the Bureau of Alcohol, Tobacco and Firearms and the Utah sheriff had raided Backwater Creek. Her father had been killed and her mother and sisters had gotten locked up for child abuse. God must have been punishing all of them, including herself, for their sins.

"You know you can't lay your ass around here and do nothing but fuckin' cry all day and night," Jordan said, yanking the bed covers off of Casey. He wasn't about to ever go broke again, but their new lifestyle and Casey's expensive pill habit was depleting their funds.

"Mikey called and sales are at an alltime low. How the fuck did it get out that you were a fuckin' polygamist cult member?" Jordan continued. Casey just stared at the wall, too weak to even pick up her pills.

"He suggested a Fuck Fest . . . you and hundreds of guys. He said it would be a huge payday and make everyone forget where you came from."

"No," Casey rasped.

"What? You ain't go not fuckin' choice, Casey. Look, money is low and shit is slow right now. You think living in this fuckin' condo is free? You think your pill habit is free? You think all those nice clothes you got in the fuckin' walk-in closet are free?" Jordan asked, taking a swig of his Mylanta. His ulcers lately had begun to bleed.

"I wouldn't know if it was free or not because I don't see a dime of the money. You choose what I eat, where I sleep and what I wear . . . remember?" Casey said rationally, still staring at the wall.

"This is gonna be your big break! Fuck those last projects that everybody had you gassed about—this is it. I'm signing the contract," Jordan said, walking out of the room.

Casey closed her eyes but the images were too painful. She could still see Dominique's battered body being degraded like an animal. She could also envision her father being shot down like an animal and her mother and sisters being hauled off like criminals.

Carissa held onto Dominique's neck and they both sobbed.

"I am still sorry I wasn't there when it all went down. I woulda fuckin' killed him. I am gonna miss your ass, girl," Carissa said through sobs. Enduring the pain of the embrace, Dominique hugged her equally as hard.

"I know . . . I know. As soon as I get on my feet, I'm gonna send for your ass. You hear me?" Dominique croaked out, her voice still hoarse.

"Make sure you call me as soon as you touch down. Don't forget to change those bandages on those burns before you get an infection. Keep those shades on so people don't be looking all up in your grill and shit . . ." Carissa rattled off a list of instructions, sounding like a mother sending her child off to summer camp.

"C'mon, you need to get inside before you miss that plane," Mr. Wonderful said, breaking the girls up. Dominique limped forward as he helped her into the terminal.

Mr. Wonderful and Carissa waited until she had gotten her ticket. Dominique turned to Carissa for one more hug. Then she hugged Mr. Wonderful.

"Thank you for getting the ticket for me and for the money. I'll repay you one day," she promised.

"Yeah, sure, baby girl. Just get ya head on straight," he said, finally seeming like he had a heart.

New York

When Dominique's plane landed at LaGuardia Airport, she felt her stomach muscles clench. It had been almost three years since she had been home. Dominique hailed a cab and gave the address of the only place she had ever felt welcome.

Huge bats fluttered around in her stomach as she approached the building. She climbed the stairs and knocked tentatively at the door.

"Who is it?" the voice called out. Dominique's heart melted and her shoulders slumped with relief.

"It's me, Mama Grady . . . Dominique." When Mama Grady pulled back the door, Dominique looked down at Mama Grady, who now sat in a wheelchair.

"Ohhh, chile. Where you been? I was so worried about you," Mama Grady cried out.

Dominique immediately began to cry as she reached down and hugged Mama Grady's neck. She had lost so much weight and she seemed so fragile.

"I'm so sorry I went away that long," Dominique cried. Closing the front door, Dominique looked at the familiar apartment. Everything was the same, except for the hospital-grade equipment scattered throughout. A large green oxygen tank sat in one corner, a portable commode in another, and the coffee table was littered with prescription medications.

"What happened?" Dominique asked, looking down at the wheelchair.

"They say I got the sugar and they had to take off one of the legs," Mama Grady explained. Dominique shook her head sympathetically.

"Sharon said she had seen you on those streets," Mama Grady announced, switching gears. Dominique didn't think she would ever have to tell Mama Grady what she really did.

"Yes, Mama Grady. I was selling my body. It was all I have ever been taught to do," Dominique lowered her head and confessed, feeling her heavy burden lift as she did so.

"Well, you gonna stay here and get better. The street ain't no place for a good girl like you," Mama Grady consoled. "I can see the God in you, chile. You ain't evil." Dominique was speechless. No one had ever said something like that to her before.

"You need something to eat," Mama Grady said, breaking the silence.

When Sharon came home, Dominique bolted upright in her chair, ready for the tirade. Sharon walked in with a scowl on her face. When she noticed Dominique, her face softened a bit.

"I was hoping you would finally come back and see her," Sharon said, sounding miffed. Sharon had listened to her mother talk about Dominique almost daily. Sharon realized that as wary of Dominique she was, Mama Grady had a special place in her heart for her.

"I'm sorry I stayed away so long," Dominique apologized, shocked to the core by Sharon's uncharacteristic kindness.

"You know she was worried sick about you. She really loves you," Sharon whispered. For the sake of her ailing mother, Sharon wanted to keep Dominique around.

"I know," Dominique managed, officially choked up.

"She is getting old and won't be here much longer. You need to do something to make her proud," Sharon said plainly. "After you left that day, I got a card from this program. The girl who started the program spoke at our church. Said her program was for sexually exploited women and girls. She was a victim herself and now she's married to a big basketball star," Sharon explained, digging into her bag for the card. "I held on to this waiting for you to come back," Sharon said, handing the crumpled card to Dominique. *My House–Myra Holson–555 Fulton Street, Brooklyn, NY 11216.*

Dominique held on to the card like it was a treasure map. Something told her this little card could be her ticket out of hell.

Jordan and Casey packed the remainder of their things that hadn't been pawned or sold for cash. Casey threw two pills into her mouth as she looked down at the eviction notice on the table.

"We wouldn't be going through this shit if you would've just got up off your ass and worked," Jordan complained, downing almost the entire bottle of Mylanta. Casey simply ignored him. "You are very fuckin' lucky that Mikey is letting you come back to New York to do this movie. Your ass is a washed-up porn queen. You better hope this 'comeback' pans out, "Jordan continued cruelly.

"You know what? You are an ungrateful black bastard.

Nothing is ever good enough. I could fuck until my skin fell off . . . it still wouldn't be good enough for you. You kill people, you beat people up, thinking about how you can benefit from it. Just like Diamond said, you are a selfish bastard! And another thing, when this movie is over and I get my money, I'm going to Utah to see my mother too," Casey railed, her words choppy and awkward.

Jordan started laughing. "You ain't shit without me. I am the only reason you ever got anywhere in this business. You are just a backward-ass white piece of shit. Don't you ever bring up Diamond or the murder again! If you do, I'll kill you with my bare hands," Jordan threatened, gripping Casey's cheeks roughly. Casey swallowed hard and yanked her head back. She needed to finish packing her bags for New York.

When Dominique stepped off the A train at Nostrand Avenue and Fulton Street, fear gripped her tightly around the neck. She hoped she didn't see anyone she knew. She hurriedly walked to Restoration Plaza to find My House. A collage of beautiful women of various ethnicities was taped on the front window. Every one of them was smiling; some even looked as if they were laughing out loud. Dominique didn't think she'd ever been that happy. Above the images a caption read: *I am a strong woman, fashioned by God to be beautiful and radiant.*

Dominique entered the building's lobby, which closely resembled a private living room. There were soft couches, oversized beanbag chairs, coffee tables and a huge, flat-screen television hanging on the wall. A few girls sat on the sofas in different stages of conversation.

A chubby girl with a beautiful face and neatly twisted dreads spoke to her first. "Hello and welcome to My House.

I'm Ambrose. How can I help you?" Her voice was melodic; her words were strung together like a soft string of pearls.

"I'm here because I need help," Dominique blurted out, the words feeling like hard marbles stuck in her throat. She didn't know what else to say.

"It's okay, here at My House we provide help," the chubby girl said as she approached Dominique.

Ambrose led her to a small office and asked her a series of questions about her history. For every answer Dominique gave—no matter how horrible her answer—Ambrose did not flinch or make a face. Dominique felt at ease talking to the girl.

They accepted her into the program and provided her with an itinerary that consisted of group therapy; one-on-one therapy; Narcotics Anonymous meetings; and a health and wellness program designed to build back the abused body.

"It's Wednesday, so our founder will be here today. She will want to meet you. She is really God's gift to women," Ambrose said with pride.

"I heard she was famous or something," Dominique commented.

"She is married to NBA star Bradley Holson. Her name is Myra and her story is so inspiring. She grew up right there in the Tompkins projects. She is really one of us; she never looks down her nose at anyone, even though she's filthy rich now. Her best friend, Quanda, comes in from time to time to lighten the mood after some of our deep and painful sessions. Quanda is a trip when you meet her, but you can't help but love her," Ambrose explained.

Dominique couldn't wait to meet Myra. She had to be an extraordinary person to fund a place like this for women.

***

Dominique anxiously awaited Myra's arrival as she sat in the group therapy session. She shifted uncomfortably in her chair as she listened to stories from girls who looked as young as fifteen. These girls had been beaten by pimps; sold by parents for crack; and raped by relatives or people they trusted. Dominique wasn't ready to share her story with so many people just yet, so she remained silent during the sessions.

When Myra walked into My House, she bore a regal presence. Although she was dressed in a simple pair of jeans, pumps and a tunic, Dominique could tell everything she wore was expensive without being flashy. The woman was truly beautiful and she seemed always to be smiling with her half-moon eyes.

"Good morning, my queens," Myra sang, flashing even, white teeth.

"I hope everyone is feeling loved and loving themselves today," Myra continued. "Today we have a few newcomers to My House so as always I will share my story with the group. For those of you who have heard it before, I hope you take something new away each time." The room erupted in applause.

Myra began her story and Dominique didn't remember blinking or breathing the entire time Myra spoke. She couldn't believe she had so much in common with Myra. Leaving the session, Dominique felt like she could conquer anything. She had enjoyed her one on one with Myra, it had made her feel special.

Dominique had been in the program for four months when her therapist dropped a bomb on her. "We are at the point in your treatment where you have to confront your past in order to move on to a better future," Theresa said. The therapist suggested she visit her mother's grave to grieve properly over her death. Next, she suggested that Dominique visit Awilda and confront her about the way she treated her. Lastly, Theresa wanted Dominique to file a police report against Jordan.

"Even if he never gets arrested, it will at least give you release from all of the things he has done to you," Theresa counseled. Dominique thought she could complete all of these steps, except confronting Awilda. She didn't think she was strong enough for that. Ambrose seemed to agree with her.

The day Dominique and Ambrose went to the Pink Houses, it had been raining buckets outside. A cold sweat broke out all over Dominique's body as she climbed out of the cab. She had literally not returned to her childhood hell in all those years. Seeing Dominique's look of horror, Ambrose grabbed her hand and they entered the lobby together. Dominique inhaled deeply and pressed the button for the elevator. When she reached the floor and stepped out into the hallway, her knees all but gave way. Ambrose had to physically hold her upright.

"C'mon, you've come this far," Ambrose encouraged. Dominique lifted the knocker and banged it three times.

"Who?" an unfamiliar voice called from the other side and suddenly the door swung open. It was a little teenage girl that Dominique did not recognize.

"Um . . . hi . . . is Awilda Branch here?" Dominique stammered.

"No. Don't no Awilda Branch live here. We just moved here two months ago so . . ." the little girl said with attitude.

"Oh, sorry," Dominique said, confused. As they turned to walk away, the door across the hall cracked open. It was Ms. Hilda, one of Awilda's old friends and neighbor for years.

"Hi, Dominique," Ms. Hilda said softly. Dominique whirled around. She always liked Ms. Hilda but never respected her. She didn't understand how that woman could have known what Awilda was doing to her and not come to her rescue.

"Hello, Ms. Hilda," Dominique managed.

"You know your aunt is gone, don't you?" Ms. Hilda asked.

"Um . . . no, gone where?" Dominique asked.

"She died a couple months back," Ms. Hilda said solemnly, shaking her head from left to right like it was the worst tragedy. Dominique lost her breath for a minute. She'd never considered that Awilda might be dead.

"How?"

"Of the AIDS they said. I'm not really sure. She had gone a little crazy for a while. I used to be able to help her at least take a bath and give her something to eat, but she started being nasty and mean and cussing all the time. You know they said that medication them doctors was giving her was 'spiramental so she was like a guinea pig. Her reactions wasn't good . . . not good at all," Ms. Hilda explained, shuddering at the memory.

Tears fell from Dominique's eyes. Ambrose hugged her and told her it was okay. Dominique figured they both thought she was crying for Awilda, but it was really out of anger. Now she would never be able to tell Awilda how much she had ruined her life.

The months flew by like days and Dominique was proud of herself for staying clean in the program. Dominique had spent the day providing services to girls who were still out on the streets. In the evening, she went to Mama Grady's, excited to share her accomplishments with someone.

One evening she walked into Mama Grady's house, and

knew right away something was amiss. No food smells wafted through the door. Despite the wheelchair, Mama Grady still slid around that kitchen and prepared food every single day. Dominique also noticed a mess of medical supply packaging on the living room floor and Mama Grady's wheelchair pushed over in a corner.

"Mama Grady!" Dominique called out, a feeling a dread washing over her. She ran through the apartment but there was no sign of her anywhere. When she walked over to the table, she found a note from Sharon. They had taken Mama Grady to Mount Sinai Hospital.

Dominique raced out of the apartment and ran as fast as she could toward the train station. She couldn't keep still on the train. When the door finally opened on her stop, she darted from the train car like a mad women. By the time she reached the hospital lobby, she was drenched in sweat. Just being in the hospital again made the hairs on her arm stand up.

"I'm looking for Ina Mae Grady," Dominique huffed out.

"She is in Cardiac Intensive Care ma'am . . . only relatives allowed," the front desk receptionist said.

"I'm her granddaughter," Dominique lied so fluidly she could've believed it herself.

"Okay . . . here you go," the receptionist said, handing Dominique the little laminated pass. She sped over to the elevators and banged on the buttons. When it came, she jumped in and walked in a circle until she got to the right floor. Walking down the corridor, she banged on the glass door until she was buzzed through.

Everything was blindingly white on the cardiac ICU. The smell of alcohol and disinfectant made Dominique gag—it smelled like death.

She spotted Sharon immediately and rushed to her side.

"Sharon, what's going on?" Dominique barked, her heart racing so fast.

"I think she is just holding on for you," Sharon said solemnly.

"What are you talking about, Sharon?" Dominique screamed, stomping her feet.

"Go inside, Dominique. You need to see her before she goes. She's waiting for you," Sharon said, tears falling silently from her eyes. Dominique swallowed hard. Sharon didn't know what she was talking about. Mama Grady was going to be fine.

Dominique moved slowly into the room, feeling like she was floating on air. Her knees buckled at the site of Mama Grady's body connected to several tubes.

"No . . . no, please . . . no," Dominique cried, bending over in pain. The heart monitor blipped a slow, steady rhythm. Dominique grabbed Mama Grady's hand and combed her fingers through the silver hair that resembled a soft bird's nest. Dominique watched her chest rise and fall with every hiss and pump of the machine.

"Please, don't leave me. I need you. I can't finish this journey without you," Dominique cried, rocking and gripping her warm hand, wishing life into her body.

"Mama Grady, I haven't said this to anyone since I was twelve years old . . . but I love you. I love you so much. Thank you for teaching me how to love myself," Dominique cried pitifully, bending in and kissing Mama Grady on her forehead.

Something on the machine began to ring. Alarmed, Dominique bolted upright, grasping Mama Grady's hand even tighter. The room filled with a cavalry of nurses and doctors. They pushed her aside to fuss over Mama Grady.

"Get her out of here," one nurse yelled. Dominique was

pushed out of the door. She ran straight into Sharon and grabbed onto her. They sobbed in each other's arms like two sisters. Finally, the doctor returned. "She is gone. I am so sorry for your loss."

Dominique screamed loud enough to wake the dead. She felt like dying herself.

Dominique sat in the back of the Abyssinian Baptist Church trying not to be angry at God. Mama Grady's home going service was beautiful. Dominique listened to the choir sing and finally felt at peace with her death.

While the pastor spoke, a man came and touched Dominique's arm, offering his condolences. He told her he had been an apprentice pastor at the church and had grown to love Mama Grady. Dominique had a hard time maintaining eye contact with him, embarrassed by her scarred face and the urges she still had to get high. The man was persistent until he had finally broken through Dominique's tough exterior. This tall, cinnamon-colored stranger with perfect teeth and the sharpest suit had softened Dominique's hardened heart by just mentioning Mama Grady's name.

Dominique returned to church every week after that. It was the thing that kept her from going out to find drugs. She had considered getting high every single day since Mama Grady had closed her eyes. Dominique had began shutting herself off from her friends at My House. The church and the new pastor had made her good enough and she didn't have to face her past like she did at My House. Dominique eventually stopped going to My House altogether. Being at the church offered her the same refuge and hope for the future as My House, she rationalized.

Dominique and Pastor Alton Camden began their courtship with the support of everyone in the church. Dominique poured herself into their relationship to keep her mind off drugs. She hid behind makeup until her scars were healed. She buried her secrets and lived out a fantasy she thought she'd never live. After less than a year, Alton had convinced her to marry him. It had been a small, intimate ceremony. Dominique did not invite any of her old friends at My House, afraid that Alton would find out about her past and lose interest in her. Instead, Dominique filled her void for Mama Grady with her new husband.

Casey swallowed three pills and chased them down with Patrón—her new sleep potion. She looked at herself in the mirror. "That bastard!" she cursed, noticing the blue and green bruise Jordan had left on her cheeks. He had grabbed her face forcefully when she refused to sign the contract for the Fuck Fest movie he wanted her star in. Casey had shuddered at the thought of thousands of men having sex with her, one after the other. But in the end, she had signed on the dotted lines. Jordan needed the money and so did she. The filming was set to start on March 10 and end on the 13, which just so happened to fall on a Friday this year. Casey hoped that wasn't an omen.

Chapter Fifteen

Healing Wounds

Whenever Brice closed his eyes, the night he saved his sister's life would play over in his head. Now, he sat vigil at his sister's hospital bedside, refusing to leave even to change his clothes. They wanted to keep her for observation and to run a battery of tests. Ciara couldn't remember much of what had been done to her, which Brice was grateful for. His mother lay next to his baby sister, smoothing her hair down and acting as if she never wanted to let her child go again. Brice jumped to attention when he heard a small knock on the door. The police officer who had been assigned to stand guard peeked his head around the door.

"There's a lady out here to see you, Detective Simpson," the officer informed.

"I'll be right back," Brice told his mother. In the hallway stood a petite woman holding a bouquet of flowers.

"I . . . I didn't mean to intrude," Bridgett Coleman said, abruptly handing him the flowers.

"Not at all," Brice said.

"I just wanted to say thank you for catching my daughter's killer," Bridgett managed, before her tears started dropping.

"And I want to thank you as well. If it weren't for the information you provided, I would have never made the connection and my sister could be . . ." Brice returned, his voice trailing off. Bridgett reached out and hugged Brice, hard. She finally had closure over her little girl's death.

Dominique watched from her car as the FBI and Suffolk County Police Department descended on her home like a swarm of bees on a hive. After they kicked through her front door, she heard loud crashes from inside. All of her possessions were being thrown around—destroyed. Dominique needed to see him being taken out in handcuffs. Then she would know it was all over.

Finally, Alton emerged with his head down and his body bent at the waist. The media trucks were capturing their footage from a distance just like she was. Dominique swallowed hard. It had taken her eight tries before she finally placed the call to the police, but she was glad she had done it. After she provided the information, the authorities began investigating Alton. During surveillance they discovered that he had been paying a crooked NYPD cop to provide him with underaged girls. Dominique cooperated with the police and helped them get up enough probable cause to secure a search warrant for the church and their home. They'd found Alton's stash of external hard drives filled with child pornography. Dominique had brought him down, and in the process, saved girls just like herself.

"You okay?" Ambrose asked Dominique.

"Yes, I am ready to confront my past and look ahead to the future," Dominique said, repeating what her old therapist had told her. Dominique had tried to run from her past, but she always ended up in nearly the same place—with another abusive man. This time she would do things differently.

***

Backwater Creek was smaller than Casey remembered. It still had that seemingly red glow from the Utah dirt. Casey bent down and ran her fingers through it. She inhaled and took in the familiar scent of burning wood stoves. There were no guards at the front gate like when she was a child and some of the houses had been reduced to piles of rubble. She walked along the dirt path until she reached the small white cross. It had been knocked over and the wood was weather beaten. She set it upright and ran her fingers over the letters that spelled out the name of her deceased son.

Casey stood on the porch of her childhood home like a stranger. After living in big cities for so long, Casey felt like she'd stepped back in time into an old Western movie. Finally, a lady came to the door. The woman was dressed in the traditional FLDS garb. "Yes, can I help you?" the woman asked.

"I'm looking for my mother," Casey said.

"Your mother?" the woman asked, confused.

"Yes, Margaret Pete."

"Oh, honey, Margaret Pete has been dead for three years now. She was one of my sister wives," the lady said, wiping her hands on her apron. The shocking news immobilized Casey, making it difficult to breathe. In a matter of seconds, she fell to the ground in a faint.

"Help!" Jordan screamed as he balled his body into a fetal position. Just as he did, he felt his ribs buckle under another close-fisted blow. Jordan felt kicks to his kidneys and genitals. Then he took a blow to the stomach. He felt like a volcano had erupted inside of him. Blood bubbled up his esophagus and spewed from his mouth involuntarily.

"That's what you get for being a kid killer, muthafucka!"

one inmate growled, spitting on Jordan as the others continued to let their blows land at will. The COs stood in the bubble and watched. They had heard all about Jordan Bleu and didn't have any desire to interfere with the inmates' own dispensation of justice.

Dominique stood up in front of the girls at My House and flashed a bright smile.

"Today, it is my pleasure to welcome you to our Stories of Survival gathering. We will hear from two victims and a police officer about the sexual exploitation of women and how it can be stopped," she announced.

Myra looked on proudly as all of the media cameras snapped and clicked. My House was getting a lot of coverage these days, which helped get the message out to the public, and especially to those women in need of assistance.

"So, it is with great pleasure that I bring our two survivors to the stage, Ms. Casey Pete and Ciara Simpson!" Dominique gushed.

Ciara held on to Casey's hand and they exchanged a telling glance. They walked out on stage, no longer ashamed of being women who had survived and eventually been emancipated from their sexual slavery.

Brice and his mother sat in the audience. A feeling of pride and sadness washed over him. Being in the presence of the My House victims, one of whom, was his sister, made Brice wonder about the girl he had raped. Was she dead, strung out or pimped out? These were all thoughts he considered. Brice wished he knew where to find her so he could apologize and tell her about My House. He wondered if that would be enough to repay what he had stolen from her.